True Nature

Books by Willow Madison

True Beginnings

True Choices

True Control 4.1

True Control 4.2

we were one once 1

we were one once 2

Existential Angst

the SAYER

True Nature

Willow Madison

Madison, Willow

True Nature (True Series, Book One)

Front Cover Design by David Colon (www.colonfilm.com); Back Cover Design by XIX (www.thenineteen.net)

This is a work of fiction. Names, characters, places and incidents are either the product of the author's imagination or are used fictitiously, and any resemblance to actual persons, living or dead, business establishments, events or locales is entirely coincidental.

This book is intended for adults only. Spanking and other sexual activities represented in this book are fantasies only, intended for adults. Nothing in the book should be interpreted as advocating any non-consensual spanking activity or the spanking of minors.

www.willowmadisonbooks.com

ISBN-13: 978-0-996-31910-2
ISBN-10: 0-996-31910-7

Author's Note

Please, read this shit for your sake, not mine

True Nature is the first book in a series that includes 2 alternative endings. All books in this series are published. I've combined elements of Domestic Discipline, Dark Romance, and D/s. It's not a typical hearts and flowers story. There are thorns and it's not for the faint-of-heart.

I know. I know.

How many times have you heard that?

Me too.

I hate this part – the "warning" or "trigger" alert. I don't really know what to say. Because I don't really know you – the reader – so I can't presume to know what emotions you'll go through with this series.

I can tell you that I had fun writing it. But I'm sick and twisted that way. In this series, I take a sweet, innocent girl (some may call my heroine a doormat…gah'head, Lucy doesn't mind) and let one helluva an Alpha try to twist her into his ultimate picture of perfection. I get tingly just thinking of all that happens to poor Lucy. But she doesn't mind this either. Oh, no, Lucy doesn't mind at all. Maybe she's just as sick and twisted as me? Sorry, you can't see me, but I'm shrugging.

Max is my Hero. Well…anti-hero *is* a bit more accurate I suppose. Maybe you'll love him. Maybe you'll hate him. Maybe you'll love to hate him. Doesn't matter. Max knows he's a bastard and he doesn't give a shit. He's found what he wants.

This is Lucy's and Max's story. It *is* a love story. A merrily, sick and twisted love story.

On board with that? Cool. Enjoy the ride.

1 Her

"Can I get a Knob Creek neat?" It's hard to keep my voice from breaking after being at the club for a while, too much dancing and yelling to be heard over the thumping music and people.

The bartender leans in over the drink-soaked bar like he didn't hear me, "That's a big order for such a little girl." Before I can respond, I don't think the dumb open-mouthed look is sufficient, he turns away.

Good. At least he got my order then. I like bourbon, it warms a spot that needs warming. It's my drink of choice when it's Saturday and I have no plans the next day. And I think it makes me sound sophisticated and mysterious; usually the finance and computer geeks in these clubs are impressed anyway. *Damn right it's a big girl drink, so there, Mr. Hot Bartender.* I need to stop talking to myself like this. *I just laughed out loud for fuck sake.*

He returns with a drink that is definitely not Knob Creek. It's pink. "On me," he says with a wink. *Who winks anymore?*

"Hey, wait a sec…This isn't mine." As I push the drink towards him, I get a good look at his hands and arms for the first time. He has olive skin, lean muscles and surprisingly manicured nails.

"I know what you ordered. This one's on me though…vodka cran." His voice is deep, no accent. *Must be from here, born and bred Midwesterner like me.*

I give the same dumb look. *Say something already.* "I'd like the drink I ordered…please." His crinkly-eyed smile is almost a laugh, probably because my voice squeaked at that last bit. Hard to sound demanding with a high voice, but I'm trying for a strong look to go with it.

"Sorry, watered-down vodka's all you're going to get." His smile goes up a little on the left and he leans in again. I can smell a hint of his cologne; like his hands, a surprising mix, musky spices and clean linens. It distracts me, disarms me in the middle of this pulsing people-pushing place to have his scent fill my nose like that. I quietly say, "Thanks," and turn around.

Looks like tonight is going downhill fast. I came out with my friends, Tracy and Laura, who are now trying to dance with what looks like brothers, really drunk brothers. Tracy is pushed against the opposite wall and staying out of the way of Brother #1's gyrating arms; Laura is laughing more than dancing, holding her sides while sidestepping Brother #2's feet.

I pass them to the steps just to the side of the dance floor. Laura and Tracy quickly join me, sharing the blow-by-blow I missed during my trip to the bar. Seems the drunk brothers are

VIP's and have a table behind the roped-off section behind us. They offered to let us sit at their table and buy us drinks and be groped while dancing. *Yippee for us. Yep, tonight is sucking.*

I usually enjoy nights out like this...the freedom to let loose, drink a little too much, maybe meet a guy or two, and dance with my friends like it's an Olympic event. But tonight feels off. Maybe it's the stress of work lately, the stress of my folks visiting next week, or the stress of feeling lonely in a crowded room...again.

Nope. I won't allow myself to wallow in this feeling. Won't let this night go without a fight. "Come on. Let's dance...and *not* with the dynamic duo." Putting my oh-so-pink drink down on a ledge, I push both Tracy and Laura back onto the floor.

I'm not a great dancer, a little too free with the jumping up and down to really get a groove thing going. At 5 feet, I still manage to take up a lot of dance floor though and soon we're screaming along with every other girl to "I will survive," a remix, but still a good mood changer. *Feeling better already.*

Tracy is a great dancer, no self-consciousness, just pure movement. Guys can't help but watch her. Laura tries hard to match her moves, but her own slightly heavier body makes her want to hide more than stand out. I end up grabbing Laura's hands and twirling her around, giving her something else to concentrate on.

Tracy has already turned down two guys trying to push their way in between us. Laura and I exchange looks. We hope we don't have a repeat of last week. A guy had put his hand on Tracy's ass, so she turned around and hit him in the stomach. We ended up leaving early to avoid more trouble.

With a few turns, I get a view of the bar again. The same crooked grin and laughing eyes are on me each time. *Maybe tonight isn't so bad.*

A slow song starts; Laura and I dance cheek-to-cheek. Tracy leaves for the bathroom to quickly avoid the guy to her left. He's a whole head shorter than her and has tried to dance with her whenever we're at Club French. Poor guy must live here waiting for his chance at the tall redhead.

A glance at the bar shows the hottie bartender talking to three girls. *At least he's not smiling at them.*

"If we dance any longer like this, I will never get a guy to ask me." Laura pushes me off. She and Tracy have been my best friends for the last two years, when we started at the same company. We met in orientation and have stuck together ever since. She is always looking for a guy to ask her for something, a date, a dance, anything.

"But, baby, I was just going to dip you," I laugh with a fake pout.

"No way...you dropped me last time! And I have to pee." Laura leads the way to the bathrooms. We pass in front of the bar. When hottie looks up, he winks at me again. *What is with the winking? Is this a new/old thing guys are doing now? Do I wink back?* Instead, I opt for raising my eyebrows and smiling halfway. *Lame-o.* I look back and see him smiling at me still, making my neck ticklish and warm.

Tracy is in line ahead of us, but moves back. "I'm gonna get a drink instead. You guys want anything?" I take their orders and head back to the bar.

Even though a group of girls are trying to get his attention, he comes right over to me. "Let me guess. Knob

Creek, right?" His eyes are a mix of green and gold or maybe it's just the bar lights making them appear cat-like.

"Yes...please," I falter. I didn't expect him to remember; the club is packed with drunk girls. "Oh, and two Greyhounds too, please." My voice squeaks again over the music. *Why is he making me want to be extra polite, like I need a bartender to like me in order to serve me a drink?*

He returns with two Greyhounds and one pink drink. No smile. "Is it just me or are you a bad bartender to everyone?" I try to make it sound like a joke.

Still no smile. "Just you. Bourbon isn't a girl's drink."

"Is that in the Bartender's Handbook?" I'm still trying to get a smile; wanna see if his eyes are the same color when they crinkle up.

"Nope, just my handbook." I only get a small smile, crooked but closed, no crinkling.

"How much for the drinks?" I match his small smile.

"On me, Lucy." He reaches across the bar and grabs my hand. "I'm Max Traeger by the way." He doesn't let go of my hand.

"How'd you know my name?"

"It was on your credit card." His hand is a little wet from the bar towel, but very warm. I feel cold when he finally lets go.

Just as I'm turning to hand a drink back to Tracy and Laura, Max asks, "Can I get your number?" I can almost see the looks they must be exchanging behind my back.

I give him Tracy's line, "How bout you give me your number instead. Girl's gotta be safe, ya know."

A small lowering of his brow makes his crooked smile seem bigger, his eyes darker. "Call me old-fashioned. I believe it's the guy's job to do the calling. If you change your mind, let me know." He turns slightly to take the order of the couple to my right, but gives me one more smile before moving away. I'm a little numb by his instant rejection. *It always worked for Tracy.*

Turning all the way around, I can see the girls are both open-mouthed too. "What was that about?" Tracy wants to know.

"Yeah, what'd we miss," chimes in Laura.

"Nothing. Just harmless flirting for free drinks. Drink up!" *Oh, well. Not meant to be my night after all.*

"I'm hungry. You guys wanna grab some food? The restaurant upstairs is still serving and last call here will be any minute," Laura loves the French faire, at least the French fries, next door.

"The kitchen will be closing in thirty minutes and the only tables available are in the bar area," the hostess shows us to a table near the empty bar. Before we can even order though, the waitress brings over fried calamari, mini burgers, French fries, and chocolate cake, "Compliments of Mr. Traeger, ladies. Enjoy."

We say, "Who?" in unison.

I follow up with, "Do you mean Max, the bartender downstairs?"

"Um, yes. He thought these items would be to your liking. Enjoy ladies. And let me know if you need anything."

The waitress walks away before we can answer, "Thank you," in unison again.

Tracy is used to getting free stuff from guys, "It's no big deal, he must have overheard us. And the restaurant is attached to the bar, so he probably gets free stuff here too."

Laura doesn't care how we got the food, she's just happy to have some so quickly, "I'm *starving*. Dig in." They take turns making fun of my goofy smiles. *I can't help it. The fries taste better somehow.*

Leaving the restaurant, I stop between the street and the steps leading back down to the bar, "You guys go ahead. I'll catch my own cab."

"Are you going back to the bar to give a great...big...thank you?" Laura giggles and makes a smacking kiss sound I hope never to hear from her again.

Tracy is laughing as they get into their cab. "Just to say thank you and leave your number you mean? You know my rule...make the guy wait for you." She says this so loudly that the group of guys walking my way all laugh and start yelling out "I'll give you my number" and "I'll give you more than my number without making you wait, sweetheart." I hurry down the stairs before they get too close.

"We're closing up, no more entries even with a hand stamp." The bigger of the two bouncers blocks the entrance.

"Can I just leave a note for someone that works here?" Both bouncers smirk at me. I bet girls leave lots of notes all the time. I feel lame, but ask for a pen and tear off a corner of a flyer on their entrance table. Folding the note, I ask them to give it to Max the bartender.

"You mean Max Traeger?" The bouncers look a little nervous, like I just said something wrong. "Ya know if you wanna go in, go ahead. You can give him the note yourself," says the shorter guy.

I feel silly enough without having to track him down in an emptying bar. "No, that's okay. Just please give him the message," I turn around quickly before they can say anything else.

2 Him

"Hey, Jimmie. What side you want me on?" I just got to the club. The music is loud. The bar is a mess. The two bartenders are running back and forth. The bussers aren't in sight.

"Thanks for showing up, Max. Tonight's been crazy with Mike out again. Take the front station...it gets the most action," he says with a laugh.

"Ha, great. Haven't tended bar in a long time and you throw me to the wolves?" I like Jimmie. He keeps his cool in a rush and doesn't lose bottles or money like some of the other guys.

After a few orders, I feel like I'm back in college. Not missing a beat with mixing drinks, opening bottles, wiping down the bar, pouring shots for smartass girls and dumbass guys.

I notice the petite blonde edging around the packed dance floor. She was up to the bar earlier with her friends, but let the redhead do the ordering. *Well, let her get a couple guys to buy them drinks.*

I like the way the blonde looks. She stands out from the other girls who are squeezed into clothes way too revealing for my taste. Bouncing, slightly frizzy curls, blue eyes, tight skirt. Can see she has a nice body, but isn't trying to sell it.

And I like the way she moves. She's not quite touching the guys she's trying to get around, just putting her right hand near their backs in case they bump her, her left arm behind her back. Looking down instead of smiling at everyone.

"Can I get a Knob Creek neat?" Her order makes me want to laugh. *Probably read it in a book and thinks it sounds grown-up.* Her voice is perfect, soft and high. *I'd like to make her squeak for real.* Name on her card is Lucy Shannon.

The confused look on her face when I set her drink down makes me smile even more. She's speechless for a second, with a slight frown, but almost said "thank you" automatically I think.

Her hands are delicate, pushing the drink back towards me, the nails a little chewed. She blushes at my response. Her thanks sounds tiny.

I keep an eye on her, hoping she'll come back up to the bar. Instead I get a great view of her tits bouncing as she sort of dances, mostly jumps in the middle of her friends. Clenching my jaw, I make out three other guys taking an interest too. *She really shouldn't bounce around like that.*

Just as two of the guys are moving closer to her on the dance floor, she starts making her way towards me again. *Nope, damn, just heading to the bathroom.*

I didn't have to stop her on her way back though. She's smiling again, white teeth almost fluorescent in the lighting. I take my chance to get her number before the night's over or some asshole goes for her first. Her response isn't good. Sounds like she's saying something for her friend's benefit; the redhead gives me a knowing smile behind her. *I don't play that game.*

Too bad, but maybe I'll see her again. I overhear them talking about heading upstairs to French Brasserie.

"Jimmie, I'll be right back." He nods my way. I take the back stairs up to the kitchen. "Hey, Manuel. How was it tonight?"

The cook thumbs-up and keeps moving around the counters. "Bueno. Estaba ocupado, Mr. Traeger."

"Good man." I clap him on the back as I leave the kitchen.

End of the night, I know the only area still serving is the bar. I see a waitress and call her over to me. "Hi, Mr. Traeger. Can I get you something to eat?"

"No, Melissa, thanks. But see that group of girls over there, just sitting down," I nod towards Lucy and her friends as the hostess is directing them to a table. "Can you send over some of our appetizers...ya know, burgers, calamari, whatever, and chocolate cake? Get 'em whatever they'd like on me."

"Of course, Mr. Traeger." I smile as I head back down to the bar for last call. *Let's see if she has good manners and stops by to say thank you.*

Sitting at the bar while the crew works around me, I enjoy the drink she tried to order. *Girl's got taste.* Brett hands me a torn piece of paper. "A blonde left this for you."

"Is she still here?" Looking around at the stragglers being herded out of the now overly bright bar, I don't see her.

"No. But I told her she could come down to give it to you herself," he adds quickly.

"All right. Brett, next time...don't take my messages. Got it?" He nods and quickly walks away.

3 Her

I open my eyes to the sun just spreading across the brick wall next door. *Must be about 6:30 then.* I love getting up early on my days off, have the whole day to myself and no plans. Well, plans, but nothing stressful. *And, bonus, no hangover. Guess not drinking bourbon paid off.* This makes me smile thinking about Max again.

I think he was in a dream I had....something about pirates in an office building and him sweeping in on a vine to the rescue. In my dream, he was shirtless, the muscles that stretched his black t-shirt last night clearly on display. *Wouldn't mind getting to see that in real life.* The middle finger of my left hand absently rubs my pussy through my sleep shorts. Laughing out loud kills the mood though. *He's probably a hairy monkey. Yep, that's how I'll picture him if he doesn't call.*

Lazy bones, get up. I run through my plans today. *Gotta clean, do some laundry and head to the beach.*

It's early, but Tracy already has a throng around her blanket. For a redhead, she's able to get a good tan and always wears a tiny red suit of some sort to show it off. Today, it's red and white polka dots. I'm more conservative in a black bikini that definitely covers my ass a whole lot more. And I plan to keep my t-shirt on while playing volleyball. I'm not exactly self-conscious of my large chest, but I've learned that guys will purposely spike the ball my way to see me jump and slide around if I don't cover up. I'm just not that into sports that I want to try that hard or risk a sand burn from a face-flop.

I know most of the people here, all friends of Tracy and a few folks from work, mostly from marketing. I'm her token human resources friend.

I walk over to Kalli, Steve, and two guys I don't know. "Hey, Lucy. Cute shorts. Maybe you can settle a bet for us. Steve says that there's going to be a corporate picnic this year at the CEO's Lake Michigan manse. Do you know anything about it?"

Kalli is actually only an intern, still finishing her marketing degree from DePaul, so I don't have the heart to tell her that she probably won't be invited. And I already know from Tracy that Steve is thinking of breaking it off long before we get to the annual summer party next month. "I haven't heard any specifics yet."

Steve introduces me to the other guys, "This is Tad and Bullet. My old Sigma Alpha Epsilon brothers. Bullet is interviewing for a spot in acquisitions Monday. Is he scheduled with you, Luce?"

Bullet is tall, at least 6'5 and lanky, with sandy blond hair and light brown eyes. He looks like he's spent the summer as a lifeguard so far. "Um, is Bullet your last name?"

"Nah, it's a stupid nickname that I can't shake." His laugh is cute, sort of stonerish and higher pitched than I expected. "Name's Billy MacIntosh."

"Right. You'll be interviewing with Brenda. She's a sweetheart, but she always asks the craziest questions to try to throw off her candidates."

"Uh-oh. Can you give me any pointers or is that considered insider trading in HR?"

I smile and laugh, taking off my white eyelet shorts and setting my bag down on Tracy's world map blanket. I can already feel sweat trickling between my tits. "I think we're cool. Let's see... One of her favorites is to ask what kind of animal in a zoo you'd like to be and why." I get the stoner laugh again. "Or if you could go back in time, when would you like to live and why? Really, I think it's because she's bored with the standard stuff. She's been doing this *forever*."

"Cool, thanks. Can I get you a beer...we have a cooler on the other side of the net?" He points beyond the game ending. Tracy is being grabbed and tackled to the sand by Josh, her on-off boyfriend.

"I don't really like beer, but thanks."

"How bout a swim then to cool off?" *Is he flirting with me?*

"Sure. I just rode my bike here, so I'm already melting." We pass Tracy and Josh as we walk to the edge of the water. Tracy's eyes are big and questioning. I roll mine at her. It's not like I'm celibate or anything. I just haven't had a boyfriend in a long while.

The water at Oak Street beach feels great, super cold with only a hint of Lake Michigan filth today. We wade out to my waist, the water only darkening the bottom of Bullet's boardshorts. "You are a shorty," he laughs.

"Good things…small packages," my patented response, with a squinty smile looking up at him.

"And cute," he says.

"Why Billy MacIntosh, are you flirting with me to get more insider info?" I try to sound like a southern belle and splash a little water up onto his stomach.

"No, ma'am, a true southern gent would never take advantage of a lady." He grabs me around my stomach and throws me over his shoulder, heading into deeper water.

"Let me down." I play pound on his back. He doesn't throw me into the water, but gently puts me down and holds me steady as a wave splashes water from just below my chest to my chin and sand shifts underfoot. "I'm going to tell Brenda to throw every stupid question she can think of at you." But I'm laughing.

I move a little away from him, though, making him drop his hands from my waist finally. He's nice looking and I certainly like how he can pick me up like it's nothing, but I don't like when guys think they can get hands-on so quickly. Not to mention that he's obviously had a few beers, so I'd rather not have him leaning all over me in an hour.

Tracy and Josh join us, making a circle in the water. She forces more flirting between Bullet and me, even making crude jokes about his nickname hopefully not meaning something sexual. I'm blushing and laughing more than flirting, but Bullet is being a good sport.

Before we leave the beach, Tracy asks if I got his number. "No, he's interviewing tomorrow. I think it would be awkward. If he gets the job, I'll see him later. If he doesn't, then maybe I'll see him with Steve sometime. No big deal." I shrug.

She rolls her eyes at me. "It's a wonder you ever get a date without me. I asked Josh to see if he wants to join us Wednesday night at Romona's."

"Tracy!" We're walking our bikes to the corner. I bump her hip with mine, "What did he say?"

"Knew you liked him. He said he'd love to." She's very satisfied with herself now.

Shaking my head, I get on my bike, "You should be in recruiting…you're very good at picking out people for others."

"You're welcome." I stick my tongue out at her and smile as we head in opposite directions.

My cell is ringing just as I am unlocking my front door. It's from an unknown local caller. Excited, I pick up, trying to get my shoes off at the same time to wipe off sand. I almost fall over, barely getting, "Hello," out while catching my shoulder on the doorframe.

"Hi, Lucy. This is Max Traeger." His voice sounds even deeper over the phone. I like that he doesn't feel the need to add 'from the bar last night.' "Did I catch you at a bad time? You sound out of breath."

No, just a klutz. "No, I just got home from the beach. Still trying to get sand off of me."

"Wish I could lend a hand." I'm blushing all the way to my ears. "I'm glad you changed your mind and left your number for me. I would hate to have had to track you down on my own." *How does his voice sound both sexy and laughing at me at the same time?*

"Well, you do know my full name already, so I figured any good detective could figure out the rest." *How did flirting become suddenly so easy for me? I was tongue tied around Billy.* "Besides, it's really more my friend's rule about not giving out numbers."

"You always follow rules." He says it not quite as a question.

"Tracy can be pretty...stubborn. But it was the least I could do since you so nicely took care of dinner for us. Thank you again."

"Sweet and good manners...a perfect package. You're welcome." I'm smiling too big to trust saying anything in return. He fills in the void, "I know this is short notice, but I have an event to go to tonight, and wonder if you'd like to go with me and have a late dinner. Are you free?"

I had plans for an early night to prepare for an earlier start to a stressful week. "Um, yeah, that sounds nice."

"Great. I'll pick you up at 7:00 then. What's your address? Or is that against the rules to give out too?"

"Haha. Yes it is, but you now have my name and number, so I may as well save your private dick the extra leg work." *Did I just say dick?* I quickly give him my Lincoln Park address.

"Oh...it's cocktail attire," he adds just after saying bye.

"Uh, O...kay...I think I have something that will work...hopefully."

"I'll see you soon, Lucy." I already like hearing my name from him. *It sounds softer with extra vowels or something.*

4 Him

I arrive a little early. Jeff, my driver, made good time around the park and there isn't much traffic on Sundays at this time. She lives in a slender three-floor building, first floor. Her door is directly off the street, behind a wood gate. *Hmm...Not very safe, girl.*

It sounds like the neighbor's dog is big at least. I can hear barking from upstairs before I close the gate. No doorbell, so I knock and wait. The door to my right opens, a small elderly woman looks out. I give her a smile and adjust my tie. She pushes a large German shepherd head back behind her leg and closes her door. *The neighbor makes a good watchdog.*

I can hear Lucy behind the door. I try not to smile before she opens. *Wow. That's some dress.* Not like last night, tonight everything is on display in a *little* black dress, tight, high, with ample view of the tits I only saw bouncing yesterday. *Hourglass doesn't begin to describe this girl.*

"Hi, come on in. I'm still figuring out jewelry and shoes. I'll only be a minute." Her smile makes up for the dress, and no caked-on makeup.

"No problem. I'm a little early." I whistle. "*Some* dress." She blushes a little and smooths her hands over the sides.

"Oh, thanks...I wasn't really sure about it. Ya know, not knowing your event and all." She keeps fidgeting.

As we walk further into her place, I can see that it's a studio. The front is a small seating area, loveseat and chair, two small windows look out on the front walkway and sidewalk. I can see her bed tucked around the corner. On the bed is another dress. I walk straight towards it.

She follows right behind, uncertain, "That was my other choice. It's a bit more sparkly." *And better*. It's a little longer, with short sleeves, small black beads, a higher neck, and open back.

Holding it up to her, "I like this one."

Her eyes get a little bigger, face frozen with a smile before slowly saying, "Oh…okay. I can quickly change." *Good girl*. She takes the dress from me and starts to head through an opening towards the kitchen and I'm assuming bathroom. She turns around quickly, and instead goes to a bedside dresser. Blocking my view, she fishes something out of a drawer and hides it behind the dress. "I'll be right back." I stop a chuckle. She didn't want me to see her underwear change obviously.

Her closet is open to my right. There are several shoes lining the floor, typical girl. I see a pair of black heels, tall stilettos. *My favorite*. She returns quickly, but stops under my appraising her up and down with an intense stare. "You're stunning." That she blushes so easily makes my pants stretch in the front a little. "I picked these for you."

Taking the shoes from me, "Thank you." She keeps looking down.

I put out my arm as she wobbles into the second shoe. Her small hand creates a barely-there pressure that I can feel down to my cock again. She grabs a pair of earrings sitting on the same dresser. "I'm ready then."

5 Her

Shit. He's early. I'm still running around trying to finish. I didn't clean my place before heading to the beach earlier, so I spent too long straightening up before getting ready.

I finish dropping my keys and lipstick in a satiny black wristlet, leaving it on a side table by the door. The neighbor dog is already barking before I can answer his knock. I sneak a peek through the hole. He looks good in a black suit, nice tie, dark hair shining. *Every first date should be like this.*

"Hi, Come on in." I move out of the way to let him in. Before closing the door, I glance outside. *Is that a town car with a driver waiting? He went all out.*

He's holding up my other black dress, the one I wore to a wedding last year for one of Tracy's cousins. The bride insisted everyone wear black so she really shined. Tracy wore lace with not much underneath. I think she told me they're divorced already.

"I like this one." I'm speechless for a second. He actually wants me to wear the dress that shows less of me? *Wow.* "Okay, I can quickly change." *Oops. I need a different bra though. Excuse me while I just sidestep ya and dig through my special undies pile to find the uber-uncomfy-push-up-convertible-bra, aka torture device.*

Returning to him, I'm still adjusting the dress in the back, making sure the low bra strap doesn't show. I see he's holding shoes. And of course, they're the most uncomfortable and high pair I own. *At least I won't be as short next to him now.*

He calls me stunning. *Never been called that before*! He holds out his arm for me. *Yep, his arms are as strong as I thought.* I stop a giggle from starting. *Calm down, dammit.* "I'm ready."

He closes the gate behind us. "You didn't have to get a car…a cab would've been fine." I feel lady-like as the driver opens the door for me.

"I don't like to wait for cabs. And Jeff here has been my driver for…what's it been, Jeff…3 years now?" He's walking around the other side already. I hear the driver respond, "Almost 4 years, Sir." Max holds my left hand on my knee for the whole ride, a constant reminder of the heat I feel being near him. My palm feels sweaty but his is nice and dry, his touch gentle.

"So what event are we going to?"

"It's a silent auction and dinner, proceeds go to several charities. I just have to stop by for a little work…shake and hold a few hands." *What kind of work does a bartender have to do outside a bar? Am I going to be sitting by myself while he serves trays of drinks?* "We're not staying long. I've made reservations for us at my favorite steak place in River North," he lightly squeezes my hand, "Hope my girl has a big appetite."

"I'm starving. Haven't eaten anything except a hotdog earlier." I smile at being called his girl. *Maybe if you play your cards right, mister.*

We pull up to the hotel. Max stops me from opening the door with a little squeeze of my hand, "Let Jeff do that."

Max got out on his side before me and a very short, blonde elderly woman in a full-length fur is calling to him from the curb, "Yoo-hoo. Max. Over here." He goes to her side and takes her bejeweled hand in both of his. I come over to stand slightly off to the side of them, feeling awkward.

"Robbie is frantic. Do you have what he needs?" She's loudly whispering up to him. Max pats her hand, then pats his left breast pocket, "Right here."

"Good, I won't have to talk him off the ledge tonight. That boy." She's shaking her head.

"You have fun tonight, Mrs. Standosh. Don't spend all your time at the auction tables." She's giggling like a young girl as he gives her a kiss on the cheek.

Turning towards me, he puts his hand on my lower back and directs me towards the doors. I squirm away from him. Just inside, I turn on him, "Are you selling drugs? Is that the 'work' you have to do tonight? I won't be any part of it...so just tell me and I'll go." I'm pissed. *Can't believe I fell for this guy.*

He's laughing at me though, "No," more laughter, "I swear to you," still laughing. His eyes are crinkling, I can see that they are a bright green, with the tiniest flecks of gold around the pupils; his lips are switching between a small smile and a crooked grin.

A large, balding man claps Max on the back, extending his hand in between us. "Max! How are you? Mother says you brought my paperwork? Please tell me you did…Stella is inside and I need to give her good news tonight." *What is going on?*

Max is still smiling at me, but turns his body towards the other man, shaking his hand. He pulls out a folded bunch of papers from his inside pocket. "Lucy, please excuse us for a moment. I'll be right back." *There's the wink again.*

I watch as Max directs the man towards a long table on the outskirts of the lobby. Their progress is interrupted a few times by various groups; Max quickly says hi and herds the man on before they can be stopped. I'm actually shaking my head a little watching.

All the dressed up people are walking up a flight of stairs to my left. I follow along slowly trying to fit in, but stop at the bottom of the stairs. Looking over my shoulder, I see Max shaking hands with the man again, putting the papers back in his pocket.

He's smiling at me through the distance, not the small or crooked smile, but a full teeth-showing showstopper of a smile this time. *How can he exert this feeling from so far away even, like I'm the only one he sees?* My knees actually feel wobbly, my hand on the stair rail steadying. *Should've eaten more today.*

6 Him

She has no idea the effect she has on the men that have tried to catch her eye, several turning to check her out as they've walked by. Her full attention is on me. *Good girl.* She fidgets and looks like she's holding onto the rail for security. Can't help but smile. *Wouldn't mind feeling that grip.*

My right hand naturally goes to the small of her back, my left arm out directing her up the stairs. "Sorry for leaving you. That was part of the work I needed to take care of tonight." Her hips roll nicely just below my hand as she climbs the steps.

"So who are you? The world's most famous bartender?" She's looking sideways at me with a small laugh.

"No…I'm not a bartender anymore," a little laughter in my voice too. "I'm a lawyer. But I don't even do much with that anymore. This was a favor for my dad. The Standosh family has been clients of the firm for a long time."

Entering a large chandeliered room, I point out Robbie hurrying over to a plastic surgeon sculpted woman, explaining that he's trying to get a quick divorce to remarry even quicker in the latest society page scandal to hit the family. "It'll probably get messy. But that's not my problem. My favor only goes as far as delivering some papers for signatures."

A waitress with a tray of champagne circulates nearby. I take two glasses for us. "Cheers. To our first date." She takes a little too big a gulp, her cheeks blooming with a flush.

"So why were you behind the bar last night then?"

"I'm part owner of the club, one of the silent partners with Lincoln Park Entertainment group. One of the guys has been out for family problems and I said I'd help. I tended bar through undergrad, so it was fun for me. And I got to meet you."

Sheepishly, her head down, grin appearing, disappearing, "Sorry for jumping to conclusions earlier."

"Oh, you mean mistaking me for a drug dealer? No problem," I move my hand up her back, feeling her smooth skin where the dress stops, I give a small squeeze to her shoulder, my fingers reaching down her chest. *She's so tiny.* "Glad to know you're such a good girl."

"I'm not a prude or anything, just don't want to be on a date with a dealer, thankyouverymuch." She clinks my glass again even though hers is empty. *Need to slow her down.*

"My favor also extends to hand holding a few people tonight, but I'll get that part over with as quickly as possible." I spot my friends at a low lounge table and walk us over to them.

One of the guys gets up, "My man, Max, glad you could make it."

One of the girls sitting looks Lucy up and down, and snottily says, "I thought you were bringing Nicole again. I liked Nicole."

I ignore her and introduce Lucy to everyone at once, "Dan and Becca, Mike and Stephie."

Mike quickly adds, "Don't mind Stephie, she hasn't had enough to drink to be nice yet." She glares at him and leaves the table. *Good, I never saw what he liked about that loudmouth anyway.*

"Lucy, I have to finish shaking a few hands. Do you mind waiting here for just a couple of minutes?"

She doesn't hesitate, "Sure. No problem," and sits in the now empty seat.

I don't go far from the table before I see one of the men I need to schmooze. I can overhear Becca complimenting Lucy's shoes and asking, "How'd you meet Max?"

"Last night at a bar," is Lucy's blunt answer.

Dan cracks up, "That's Max." Becca doesn't say anything more.

"So how do you all know each other?" I can see Lucy in a reflection from a mirror over the bar, she keeps looking my way.

Dan answers for them, "From law school. Well, Max, Mike, Stephie and I went to Northwestern together; Becca's been my ball and chain for about as long."

Becca slaps his shoulder, "See if I ball you tonight." Lucy laughs with them, a high and sweet sound that matches her voice. My friends go back to talking quickly and without Lucy. She gets up from the table, but I can't hear what she mumbles. I'm saying only the minimum to the two older men next to me, hiding my concentration on Lucy.

She beelines for a group a few feet away. I can no longer see her in reflection, so I move for a more direct sightline of her. A girl squeals loudly and grabs Lucy in a bear hug, clearly a little unsteady; I assume she must be tipsy already. She is obviously introducing the guy who has his hand on her ass. The guy goes to grab Lucy around her hips too.

The heat in my stomach is instant. Lucy turns and steps away, putting her hands out in protection. The move causes her to twist her foot a little, catching herself on a chair back. This guy continues to reach out and touch her arm though.

I excuse myself from the two men. Taking long strides, my right hand in a tight fist, I am quickly by Lucy's side. She backs into my chest as she's turning further away from the guy and girl. I put my arm around her back, holding her left arm gently, closing my other hand around her right arm to steady her. I force a smile through a clenched jaw, eyes steely, silently challenging this asshole to try to touch her again.

"Oh, Max, there you are. Are you all done? Christine, it was nice seeing you…" She trails off as I allow her to turn us both away, walking back towards the table of my friends.

I stop her halfway and turn her to face me, reluctantly releasing her arms; the hold had pushed her tits out nicely. "Friends of yours?"

She lightly laughs, "Not really. Just someone I recognized in this crowd."

"He seemed friendly," I try to keep my voice from sounding too gruff. She nervously laughs a little more.

"Are you all right? I saw you twist your foot there." I take advantage of the opportunity to look down her tiny frame, my hands itching to wrap around her waist tightly.

"I'm fine. It was nothing...just not used to such high heels." She pats my chest.

"I didn't like the way that guy grabbed you."

"No, it's fine. He's just not somebody I know really...just a drunk idiot," she answers like I had asked a question.

"I shook enough hands. No need to stay longer. Let's go before the auction starts." *Or I lose my cool with another guy hitting on you.* My hand in place on her lower back again, we walk towards the doors. *I gotta keep my temper tonight, don't want to scare her off.*

Jeff is waiting for us. He opens the door for her. Lucy gives him a big smile; clearly she's not used to this treatment. It feels natural to hold her hand in mine again, our fingers intertwined. Brushing my thumb lightly across her knuckles, the smallness of her causes a strain to my cock. Watching her legs open ever so slightly, the movement making the scent of her perfume linger on the air, isn't helping either. I resist the urge to adjust my pants, but don't look away from her smooth, glowing legs as they close again and rub against each other slightly.

"Who's Nicole...your ex?"

Fucking Stephie; Mike really needs to keep her on a leash. I explain that she's just a friend of sorts, "I have a lot of events throughout the year, from my connection with the LPE Group as well as the law firm. Nicole was never my girlfriend but she did look great at these black-ties." Lucy gives a small frown to this, but says no more. *A little jealousy showing maybe? Good. We're like-minded then on that note.*

7 Her

At the restaurant, everyone seems to know him. *Well, he did say this was one of his favorite places.* The hostess treated him like a returning king though. Our waitress starts to hand us thick menus, but is interrupted by a squat, round man with a white jacket and red cheeks. He is exclaiming in an Italian accent, "Mr. Max doesn't need a menu," while double cheek kissing Max who has stood again. "I have the finest Fiorentina steak just for you…and your bellisima lady." The chef kisses my hand. I'm hiding a bigger smile when he pats Max on his shoulder and adds, "I'm glad you finally bring a date here."

"Thanks, Paulo." Max makes a little small talk, the chef kind of hard for me to follow with his thick accent though. As Paulo walks away, Max orders a bottle of wine and salads for us. It dawns on me when the waitress returns with the wine that he didn't ask what I'd like to order. *Well, I don't have a menu anyway.*

"You were at the beach earlier?" He asks while pouring more wine into our glasses.

"Yeah, it's become my standard Sunday routine since the weather's been so nice." He has this way of looking so intensely at me, almost uncomfortable, almost…too hot. I find myself looking down at my hand in my lap to avoid fidgeting under his scrutiny.

"That's nice. Almost every morning I run the path around the lake, but usually before the crowds kick in. I love the beach, but can't stand the crowds anymore." And now I can't get the image of him sweaty and running shirtless out of my head. *Down girl, damn…think of the hairy monkey.* I almost laugh out loud.

"What's so funny?" He's smiling and leaning in a little.

"Oh nothing. I'm just…not that athletic is all. I admire anyone who has the determination to stick to a workout routine, though," I try to recover.

"Maybe you're not properly motivated is all," his crooked grin distracts me again. I'm just starting to feel the effects of the wine when the waitress thankfully brings over some bread and salads.

"I play beach volleyball sometimes. My friend, Tracy, she was with me last night…she's really good. I just try to avoid getting hit by the ball or making too many mistakes."

"Was she the redhead from last night?"

"Yeah," and I realize that I'm a little irked that he remembers her. *He didn't even say anything to her.* "She and Laura are my best friends. We work together. Well, for the same company. They're in the marketing department and I'm in HR," I babble to avoid hearing him say more about Tracy first. Surprisingly, he doesn't ask more about what I do for a living, the standard first date "20 questions" sort of thing.

Instead, he changes the subject. "Did you grow up around here?"

"Yeah. I'm from a small town in Indiana, more corn than people. How bout you?" I smile at his hand covering mine on the table.

He keeps moving his hand to touch me in small ways, only briefly though, brushing hair off my shoulder, rubbing my fingers holding the wine stem on the table, feeding me a small tomato when he saw I really liked them. For some reason, I don't mind all his touching. *Maybe because he doesn't linger?*

"I'm from here. Lived most of my life in a high-rise near the lake. More El tracks than corn." He laughs at me.

"I liked being from a small town, but I don't think I could ever live in one again." I try to take small sips of the wine; between the champagne earlier and not enough food, I am feeling the effects too quickly.

"Not even when you have kids?" He's looking intensely through me again.

How odd he is. "Maybe then." *Most guys wouldn't dream of bringing up having kids on a first date.* I smile back at him. I have to ask what I've been dying to know. "So...how old are you?"

He laughs at my abrupt change of subject. "I'm 35." He leans forward. "And you, young lady...how old are you?" His eyes are crinkling at me.

"26." I like our age difference. I actually thought he was a little younger than that. I tend to date guys older than me.

"Ever been married?" A few guys I've dated have been divorced and bitter, dating too soon after a tough breakup.

"Not yet." He's still crinkly-smiling at me. *He is odd.*

The giant steak arrives, and our conversation turns to the meal and food likes and dislikes in general.

"Thank you for dinner. It was delicious." We're heading towards the car; his driver is leaning against it a few feet away. Max suddenly grabs my arm and pulls me around to the side of the building, just out of reach of the street light. "Hey..." but I'm silenced by his right hand cupping my chin and ear, his left hand flattening against my ribs as he gently pushes me back against the wall.

I can feel the brick pressing into my skin where the dress is open in back, cold and rough. His kiss is slow, tender...firm. His lips are warm, tongue smooth and flat, filling my mouth. I can't even feel my own tongue; he takes my breath away with each of his own. He continues pressing, but moves his face inches away. "Ready to go home?" He has a crooked grin again, with a twinkle in his eyes now.

I can barely get out a breathy, "Yes."

The night air is cooler. Hard to believe next week will be the Fourth. As I'm opening my gate, my left hand feels chilled after the enveloping warmth of his hold in the car again. "I'll be right back, Jeff." *Phew. He's not thinking that he's coming in.* Many a second date has been refused after an awkward goodnight at the first one.

I've never been able to have a one-night stand, despite Tracy's attempts to make them happen on my behalf. And a guy who tries too quickly to get inside my pants, just isn't the guy for me. *Ya gotta work to earn that privilege.* I'm laughing silently to myself.

His hand is on my lower back again. *Amazing how quickly I've gotten used to his touch.* My face, back, arms, hands seem to tingle from his touch all night. I'm smiling as I turn towards him with my key in my hand. He surprises me by taking it and inserting it in the lock for me before opening the door slightly. But he doesn't step inside.

"You should lock the deadbolt, too." His jaw is a little more set.

"Tell my landlord. It sticks on me too often."

The stern look deepens a little, but he changes the subject, "I hope you had a nice night tonight."

"I had a great time." *Kiss me, kiss me, kiss me!* "Did *you* have fun?" I ask a little challengingly, tilting my face up.

He takes my chin in between his thumb and fingers, tilting my head back a little more. My lips are already parting as he bends down. Gently, slowly, firmly...just like the first kiss. The warmth of his breath fills my mouth, making me more lightheaded. He's still holding my chin when we stop kissing, our faces inches apart. He looks back and forth between my eyes before letting go.

"I'd like to see you again. Soon."

"I'd like that too." I answer a little too quickly, my voice extra high.

"Good. Wednesday. We can meet downtown around 6:30."

"Oh...Sorry. I have plans Wednesday..." I trail off, a dark look drifting across his eyes. "Another night this week...Thursday maybe?" I try for up-beat to chase the look completely away.

He smiles but his eyes don't pick up the message, still darker, "Okay. Thursday then. 6:30. The corner grille on Chestnut and Michigan." He kisses my nose before turning away.

He takes two of the steps down towards my gate before turning around, "You were beautiful tonight. Thank you again for such a nice time, Lucy." I can feel my cheeks burning. Hopefully he can't see how much effect his words have on me in the poor lighting.

"Thank you, too." My smile is clearly in my voice. I turn quickly and shut the door. Sighing and giggling at the same time as I turn on a light. I wait till I see the car pull away before closing my blinds.

8 Him

Wednesday, the night I wanted to meet up with her again. *Hmmm, wonder what her plans might be tonight.* I rub my tense neck; the frown I've been wearing all day starting to wear on me. I haven't been able to stop thinking about this girl....the way she smiled, the feel of her skin and hair, the sweetness of her mouth...the way she looked down at her hands over dinner.

I haven't been this excited about a girl in a long time...*hell, since Natalie*...and that was almost 5 years ago. Dan reminded me of that over lunch yesterday. He kept trying to get details about Lucy to see how serious I am. I played it off, but I think he saw through me. He kept telling me to take it slow. *Like I need advice from him.* He moved in with Becca after that first semester.

But he does have a point. Things ended pretty badly with Natalie. I need to be sure about this girl before I make any real moves.

I keep going over our date in my head, how she responded to me. There's definitely something there. *She may have a few bad habits to break,* I smile thinking of this, *but she's really a sweet girl. And that body!* My cock stirs just thinking about her.

I look at my watch, it's 8:30. *Let's see how sweet she is.* I call her, but only get voicemail. Her voice is as soft and high as I remember. My pants get a little tighter again. I hang up without leaving a message. *Bad habit #1. She should've answered her phone.* I sigh heavily, a cross between a sigh and a growl really.

Time to concentrate on something else again. The piles of paperwork delivered this afternoon sit on my coffee table. LPE business, rental agreements, renovation plans, and hiring policy changes I recommended last month all wait for me to stop thinking about a girl I've just met. Pouring a glass of Glenlivet, I absently eat Malnati's pizza and dig into the pile, the Cubs in the background.

9 Her

Coming out of the bathroom stall, I see I missed a call from Max. I don't have any new messages though. *Hope he's not cancelling our plans.*

Tracy is still talking through the door of the other stall. "...and I told Josh that I can't go with him to a cabin in the woods next week. It's the Fourth of Juu-ly and I need to part-tay with my girlfriends." She's already a little tipsy. *Hell, so am I.* Italian wine really goes to my head fast.

I hand her a paper towel, "Bet he liked that. Didn't you promise him last year that you'd go away with him this year if you guys were still together?"

"So?" She puts a fresh coat of lip gloss on. "Besides, we haven't been together the whole year...so it doesn't count." She sticks her tongue out at her own reflection. "And it's his roommate's party...it'd be rude not to go."

I laugh. "Well, the fireworks just wouldn't be the same without you. So I'm glad you're blowing him off."

"No, I told you. I *won't* be blowin him off silly, that's why he's mad." She slaps my butt as we leave the bathroom laughing.

This is our tradition. Get together on hump day, eat too much pasta at the small Italian restaurant around the corner from our office, and complain the next day that our fuzzy heads must be somebody else's fault for ordering too many carafes of Chianti.

We also love the free cheesy breadsticks and tiramisu that "Romona" sends to our table. Her real name is Rosa, but she and her husband didn't change the name of the restaurant when they took over, so we always call her Romona to tease her.

Tracy pushes me into her chair, between Josh and Bullet, and takes mine a little further down across the table instead. She's anything but subtle.

Laura has been flirting with Steve since he didn't invite Kalli. She's hopeful that this is a permanent thing, but I can see that he's really not into her that way.

Maybe it's something I've picked up being in HR, a recruiting specialty, I'm able to get to the heart of a person quickly, see what makes them tick. I take the opportunity to assess Bullet. *Gotta start calling him Billy, can't take him serious with that nickname*. He's above average looking, but not my usual type, last blond I dated was in college I think. I have my type. Max instantly pops into my head. *Tall, dark, broody.*

Ahem. I snap myself back to the table. Tracy and Josh are arguing over a six-way split of the check, "Guys, it's family-style, so why don't we all just split it equally?" Is Bullet/Billy's suggestion. *He's a real peacekeeper.*

He does smell nice too, like a scent I'm used to. "Thanks again, Luce, for your help with my interview. I'm supposed to hear something by Friday...unless you know I didn't get the job already...in which case," he play rubs his nose, sniffing and leaning back, spreading his arms wide, and landing one arm on the back of my chair. "Aah, ya know, that's cool." *And he's funny.*

"I'm sure you did fine, but I really don't know where that team is at with the position. I'll keep my fingers crossed for you," crossing fingers on both hands in front of his face. *Yeah, he's okay.*

Tracy has been trying to get us love-crossed all night, suggesting future foursomes. I think we're booked until Christmas in her mind. She's working on Steve now, trying to get him to take Laura home tonight. Poor Laura is shrinking in her chair, but not saying no.

I glance again at my phone, realizing I haven't put it away since the bathroom. *What would I do if he called again right now?* Smiling, I know I'd be happy to juggle that problem.

I haven't been able to stop thinking about Max for the past two days. He monopolizes my dreams. I have even been daydreaming about him, imagining his hands on me again with those small touches. My boss hasn't noticed, but work has been the last thing on my mind lately.

Outside, everybody's waiting for cabs. Josh is pawing at Tracy and they take off together in the first one. Laura lives my way, so we're going to share the next one, despite Tracy's attempts to pair us all off tonight. Billy yanks my sleeve, "So think we can get together sometime, grab a bite to eat or something...lunch even?"

"Um, sure, that'd be nice." His hesitancy is just what I don't like about guys my own age. I can't help but compare him to Max...*so decisive.*

I glance at my phone, still showing no messages. *But maybe he didn't mean to call me after all and just hung up before it went to my voicemail?* Billy is asking me about Saturday, "We can meet early, around 11, bike around the lake, then grab a bite to eat?"

"That sounds nice." *Is that all I can say?*

He's pulling out his phone, "Give me your number, I'll call you Saturday morning to firm up a spot to meet." I give him my number, but wonder why. *He's gotta see that I'm not very enthusiastic.*

Laura babbles about Steve in the car, alternating with questions about Billy and our date. "Maybe we can make it a double date if Steve asks me out too?"

Wishful thinking my friend, but I just shrug and hug her as I get out, leaving my portion of the cab fare with her.

10 Him

I have my back to the door, but there's a good view of everyone entering from the mirrored cabinets behind the bar. She comes in just behind a couple, looking around before she spots me on a barstool. I glance at my watch. S*he's 17 minutes late.*

I don't turn around, enjoying watching her walk up to me. Tight black skirt, not too short but showing off her legs, short sleeve white top showing a small amount of cleavage, hair pulled tightly back. She puts her hand on my left shoulder. "Hey stranger. This seat taken?" She sits on the barstool before I turn around, her knees brushing against my side. "Oh, wait. Is someone sitting here?" She points to the glass of red wine in front of her.

"No, that's for you. This place fills up quickly for happy hour, so I took the opportunity to get you a drink and save you a seat at the same time." I place my hand on her leg.

"Very thoughtful of you." She takes a sip, "This is yummy. What is it?"

"A Côtes du Rhône blend. One of my favorites."

"Do you know a lot about wine, Max?" *Two good signs...she hasn't moved away from my hand and no bullshit for ordering a drink for her.*

"Sort of a family preoccupation really. My dad's family came from wine country, back in Italy, long time ago, but the tradition of enjoying wine is alive and well today." I clink her glass, "Salute, bella."

"Cin cin," she responds.

"Nice... Have you been to Italy?"

"Too briefly. With my college roommate and her family. I haven't travelled nearly as much as I'd like. How bout you?"

She hasn't stopped smiling, leaning on the bar with her whole body turned towards me. I remove my hand from her leg for a second. She crosses her legs, left over right, skirt rising a little higher, offering more of a view. I return my hand, rubbing my thumb across the top of her knee, spreading my fingers fully across her exposed skin. She lowers her head, but keeps smiling.

"...and I still try to get to Italy once a year if I can get away from work. My dad really spoiled us with a love of travel." I haven't even paid attention to what I'm saying, I'm so distracted by the liquid electricity of touching her.

We talk more about travel, mine mostly about places I've been, hers about places she'd like to go. The conversation is easy. The whole time, I keep my hand on her; she tentatively responds now and then by placing her hand on my arm.

The bartender interrupts to ask if we'd like anything more. I answer before Lucy, "Two of the same, thanks. Do you want to get some food here, they have pretty good burgers...or go someplace else?" I ask as the bartender pours more wine into our glasses.

"Um...here's fine."

"Can we also get two burgers...cheese on yours? ...Okay, no cheese, and an order of curly fries? Thanks." The bartender walks away to add our order to the computer.

"Ya know...that's the second time you've ordered for me...?" Her head is tilted to the left side, her lips pressed together but still smiling, eyes narrowing a little. *Here we go*.

"Is that a problem?" I keep my voice low and calm, still rubbing her knee. I resist the urge to swallow hard, keeping her eye contact.

She continues to look at me narrowly before slowly responding, "No...I guess not... Just not used to a guy...ya know...being that..." She's clearly out of her element here, shrugging with each pause.

"What? That decisive, take charge?" I try these words out, testing her reaction again.

"Um...well, yeah." She gives a little shake of her head and small laugh, "Most guys don't want to make any decisions...ya know...leaving all the choices of a date up to a girl...at least most guys I've known."

"Guess I'm not most guys then." I tip my drink to her. Her smile remains tight, but her response so far is good. "And some girls would take offense at a guy ordering a nice dinner for them..."

"Guess I'm not most girls then." Her hand goes to my arm again. *A very good sign.*

"No, you are definitely not." She returns my big smile.

We're off to a good start.

11 Her

He holds the door open as I walk outside. Looking at my watch, *I can't believe it's 11:00.* We talked and laughed for so long, I completely forgot about my early meeting tomorrow.

"Does that thing work?" His eyes twinkle as he indicates my watch.

"What?" My face actually hurts from smiling so much.

"I just thought maybe that's why you were late tonight...that I need to get you a new watch." He continues smiling and twinkling, but his jaw is more squared.

"Oh...yeah...sorry. My boss likes to talk a lot and I couldn't get out of the office on time. And you might as well know now that I'm habitually late. My friends all make fun of me for it." We walk arm in arm towards Jeff across the street.

"I'd appreciate you being on time in the future, Lucy." His crooked grin only makes his jaw appear even harder from my sideways glance. He smiles more and winks at me as he walks around to the left side of the car.

"Good evening, Lucy," Jeff has the door fully open for me. I'm too distracted thinking of a response to Max though to do more than smile at Jeff's politeness. I feel chastised. He didn't say it jokingly. He said it bluntly. *He meant to chastise me?*

And the strangest thing is, I'm not angered by this. He was so soft-spoken, matter-of-fact...*like a boss telling me what to do*. And I'm not angry. *Huh.* I can't say how it makes me feel, just strange.

By the time we're pulling away from the curb, I'm unsure if I should respond to his comment after all. He thankfully changes the subject, "My friend, Dan, you met him and Becca the other night...it's his birthday tomorrow. Becca is throwing a not-so-surprise party for him, she does this every year. I'd like you to go with me."

"Sounds like fun. So long as it's not black-tie again." I squeeze his hand over my knee.

"Definitely not."

Our goodnight kiss is just as steamy. Same routine...opening my door, but not trying to come in. I lose track of time in his kisses, lips travelling from my cheeks, lips, neck, lips. I feel the heat of his breath on my face, the pressure of his hands on both sides of my ribs.

He pulls away after a final kiss on my cheek. "I'll pick you up at 8:00 tomorrow." He squeezes me a little more, tickling a little. "8 sharp." His lips play with a smile, one brow cocked. I just grin in response and go inside.

12 Her

"I'm so tired," I mumble through a yawn while in line for a second Grande coffee this morning with Tracy.

"You look it too." She gives me a toothy smile as I push her away. "You know you're beautiful." She bumps my hip in return.

It took forever to fall asleep, then I woke up several times with dreams of Max lingering. "I couldn't sleep last night."

"Thinking of the bartender?" Tracy drips sarcasm on the last part.

"I told you, he's not a bartender."

"I know, I know...but it was because you were thinking about him, right?" Tracy knows me too well. I pinch my lips together and squint at her in answer. "So you have another date with him tonight? That was fast."

"Well, it's a friend's party, so I think he just wants someone to go with..." I don't know why I'm feeling defensive about Max. Maybe because Tracy keeps making jokes about him and talking up Billy every chance she gets.

We stop to finish chatting in the hall outside my shared office. Lucky for me, my boss is taking a long weekend with her husband. *So my tired ass can coast a little today.*

"Hey. What's that?" Tracy pushes past me into the office. A red box with a bow is sitting on my desk. I open the attached card. Tracy reads over my shoulder, "Looking forward to spending more time with you. M."

Inside, the box is marked Cartier. "Is that real?" Tracy's jaw is wide, I'm too stunned to take the simple watch out of the box to look at it closer. Tracy takes it out for me and examines the front and back, "Sure looks real." She whistles a little, "Nice!"

Kevin, my officemate, comes in. "So whatdja get?" Tracy holds it out for him, he whistles too. "Girl, I was tempted to read the card, but I waited for you. I was itchin to know if that was Cartier red. Who's M?" He raises his eyebrows and flips his wrists several times while holding the card. I can feel my blush deepening as I hold the watch against my wrist.

"Max...her bartender," Tracy answers, pushing me again.

"Lordy, girl, you have got a *serious* drinkin problem if your bartender sends you goods like that." He's fanning his face playfully with his right hand. I just laugh, still a little too stunned by the gift to trust my voice. "Put it on, put it on. Let's see how it looks." Shakily I replace my old watch with the new one on my left wrist. "Ooh...it fits perfect too." Kevin squeals, clapping his hands, "My boyfriend gave me a new

wok for my last birthday. You hold onto this Max, girlie."
Kevin goes over to his desk.

"I can't believe he got me this," I finally find my voice.

"It's crazy expensive," Tracy is still staring at the watch
as she moves my arm closer then farther away. "Makes me
think of the old saying...about a guy expecting something for
expensive gifts," she tickles my sides as she says this.

Pushing her away, laughing, "Well, we'll just have to see
about that…"

"Slut." She tries to tickle me again but I move back with
my arms out.

"Takes one, baby..." We're both laughing.

"Maybe you won't always be late anymore," Tracy says
from the hall. I didn't tell her about that part of the date.
Hmmm... That same strange not angry feeling comes over me
again. This time, without wine, I have a name for it though.
Lust. I shake my head to get this thought out of it.

13 Him

She looks great. Her hair is down, curls bouncing with the motion of opening the door, long blue dress with tiny straps brightening her blue eyes even more, cleavage pushed up a little, but not slutty. I glance at her arm and frown.

I put my hands on her waist and kiss her hello, "You don't like my gift?"

"Oh, God no...It's not that..." her hands move to the sides of my arms, "I just think...it's too much."

"Why don't you let me decide that? I wanted you to have it." I see the box sitting on the coffee table. Taking her hand, I walk over to the it, take out the watch and put it on her left wrist. "I want to give you nice things. And I want you to accept them from me." I tilt her chin up, "Please."

"I still think it's too much...." She looks back to the watch then me, "But...thank you, Max. It is really beautiful." As she puts her arms around my neck, my hands travel to her lower back, brushing her ass, feeling the outline of the top of her thong. I resist pinching her round bottom as we kiss deeply.

She grabs a purse and opens a lip gloss tube, looking in a mirror by the door. "You don't need that. You're beautiful without so much makeup." I stand behind her with my arms around her waist again, looking intently at her face in reflection. She starts to say something in protest, opening the gloss again. "Besides, I want to be able to kiss you often tonight without looking like *I'm* wearing makeup."

She twists her lips and wiggles her nose, but finally puts the gloss down. "Okay, you win."

"Good girl." And I kiss the top of her head, breathing in the vanilla and orange blossoms scent of her hair.

Dan and Becca's place isn't far from Lucy's, so we walk hand in hand. I smile that in flats, Lucy's head doesn't even come up to my shoulders, "I like how tiny you are next to me."

"Small packages..." she looks up at me with a big grin.

"Well...not *all* of you is small." She slaps my shoulder playfully in response. "I meant your smile."

"Sure you did."

"You do look great in that dress."

"Thank you." She's all smiles again.

We reach the brownstone and enter with another couple I know as friends of Becca. "Wow," is Lucy's instant reaction to the dramatic foyer. Becca painted it all black to showcase her large art pieces even more. "Yeah. Becca really likes the drama. She's a buyer for private art collectors, so she goes a little crazy with art everywhere."

"It's really impressive."

"Thanks." Becca just entered the foyer, finished with air kissing the other couple and directing them towards the living room. "Max here doesn't like anything that isn't sleek and modern, so he can't appreciate fine taste like mine, dahrling." She one-arm hugs Lucy, who seems pleased by the immediate welcoming nature of Becca. "The birthday boy should be here any minute. If he isn't fucking late again this year. We're waiting in the living room this time." She waves us towards the room to the right of the stairs.

"Does she really expect us to yell 'surprise' at Dan when he comes in?" Lucy asks with a giggle as we walk away.

"Yes...yes, she does. And she'll put you in charge of cake cutting if you don't. Made that mistake two years ago."

The living room is already packed with friends. Most from here, a few from out East where Dan grew up. I spot Mike and Stephie sitting on the sofa and head in their direction.

"Hey!" Mike high-fives me and smiles at Lucy, "It's Lucy, right?" He shakes her hand as she nods.

"You remember Mike and Stephie from last week?" She smiles and only nods. I think she's waiting for Stephie to be rude again.

Mike must have warned Stephie to be nicer though. She smiles up at Lucy and puts her hand out. "Glad you could make it. This party is one of the highlights of the year."

Lucy relaxes her shoulders. "This place is amazing. I don't think I've ever seen this much art outside a museum."

The walls and tabletops are covered with a mix of contemporary and baroque pieces. Mike stands up and lets Lucy take his seat next to Stephie.

"Yeah, Bec has a great eye for it. She'll give you a tour later. The best pieces are upstairs." I'm glad Steph is being nice tonight. She is either hot or cold with people. *For some reason, though, Mike really loves her.*

"I love to check out other people's houses. I am a secret peeping-tom, looking in windows when I can." Lucy is laughing at herself.

Stephie sits up more, almost spilling her drink, and laughing. "Oh my God...I thought I was the only one! Mike always makes fun of me. I *love* when it's night out and people don't close their blinds and I can see how they've decorated."

"Me too!" They both erupt in laughter. Lucy's face scrunches up, and she puts her hand over her lips to cover her open mouth laugh, her tits more visible from my angle and shaking nicely. I look around to make sure no one else is enjoying my view though. I make a mental note to talk to her about how she dresses when she's not with me. She looks up and sees me staring down at her. She self-consciously puts her hand over her cleavage and pulls her dress up a little, giving me a small smile.

And it's in this moment, that I fully realize how much I like her. I'm a little shocked at how quickly I've developed such a strong feeling for her.

"Max. Get Lucy a drink...rudeness." Stephie grabs my forearm and shakes me a little.

"We'll be right back." Mike grabs my other arm and pulls me towards the kitchen. I just wink at Lucy as I let him drag me away.

"Two champagnes, please," I tell the woman behind the island, set up now as a full bar. Becca goes all out, hiring bartenders and waiters to circulate and keep the party going into the late hours.

"So...wow...you brought a date this year." Mike slaps my back as we wait for our drinks. "You must really like this Lucy?"

"I do." I know I should hide my goofy smile from him, he'll not let me live it down for weeks, but I can't help smiling bigger.

"Look at that puppy love look." He rubs my hair, having to reach up over his own head to do it.

I smooth my waves back down. "She's special." I already had this conversation with Dan. But Mike isn't as cautious as Dan, he's more willing to go with the flow and I know he won't try to put the brakes on how I'm feeling right now.

"She's *hot*." He laughs at his own joke.

For a second I forget that he's one of my best friends, a brother to me, and I clench my fist before relaxing again. I respond with a grin, "She is that."

"Have you...?" He makes a grinding motion with his hips against the bar.

I just laugh and push him away. Our drinks are set on the bar, so I pick up two flutes and head back into the living room before he can question me more.

Becca is just coming in, waving her arms. "Okay everybody...Quiet. He's coming up the walk."

Someone hits the lights, the room darkens to only candlelight. I find Lucy on the sofa and pull her hand to stand up next to me. We quietly clink our flutes and take a sip. I put my arm around her waist and she crowds in closer to me, putting her free hand on my back. I can't believe how happy I feel with her at my side, her smallness making me stand even taller. *I probably do look like a lovesick puppy*. But I keep smiling, and she smiles looking up at me too.

I lean down and whisper, "Surprise," into her ear. She shivers at my side, her nipples pushing against her dress. She only bumps my back in response though, smiling into her glass and looking around.

"Surprise!" Everyone yells as the door opens and Dan walks in, arms already out for the cheers. His smile is huge and wide open. Becca runs forward and grabs him around the waist. He dips her and kisses her to more cheers.

"He's such a ham." Mike leans over to say to me quietly over Lucy's head. Dan says he doesn't want a party every year, but we both know he loves it. We just laugh whenever he denies it.

After getting more hugs, handshakes, and pats on the back from the people closest to the doors, Dan makes his way over to us.

He puts his arms out and hugs all three of at once, smooshing Lucy in the middle. She's laughing and ducking down.

"Did you assholes bring a gift this year?"

Mike feigns looking hurt and shocked. "What? Becca said no gifts. You're too old to deal with the excitement." Dan back-hand slaps his stomach and Mike slaps his head. They're laughing harder as Becca comes over to drag Dan away for the toast.

He stands on an ottoman, with Becca trying to push him down. He waves her off and she comes to stand next to Mike who puts his elbow on her shoulder. She stands with her arms crossed, laughing though.

"Friends...Brothers...Cubs Fans…" He gets a few boos, cheers, and napkins thrown at him. "And my be-A-U-tiful wife!" Hoots and hollers now. Becca curtsies, Mike almost falls over from leaning on her. Everyone laughs, he's always been a clown. Stephie pulls his shirt back and he sits next to her again.

"On this the blessed day of my birth," Dan bows his head and continues through the boos and cheers, "I am reminded of a poe-em." All boos now, Becca is shushing people, but laughing too. Dan clears his throat loudly. "There once was a man named Dan," he lifts his brows wickedly to all hoots now. "Dan the man lived in a van," dramatic pause, "until he met...the ravishingly rapacious Rebecca." The hoots take a second to die down now. Becca is covering her face and laughing harder. "The HOT Rebecca tamed this nomad man Dan," more hoots, "and set up house...here…" He opens his arms and almost falls off the ottoman. He raises his brows up and down once more to cheers when he rights himself again. "So all you fuckers can gather round... once a year!" Everyone laughs and cheers, he play acts falling into the arms of his adoring fans. Becca pushes him away when he tries to slobber kiss her face. Everyone cheers a glass to him.

"The party is officially started now." Mike says from the sofa, standing up and downing his glass. "Drink up, ladies." Lucy clinks glasses with Stephie and they both down their drinks, too.

"Did he really live in a van?" Lucy asks us, laughing.

"For one week, he was in between campus housing." I answer laughingly, also downing my drink.

"Man, do you remember how *bad* that van smelled?" Mike and I both laugh at his comment. "More drinks. To the bar…" He takes Stephie's glass and I take Lucy's, heading back towards the kitchen.

Dan joins us and is immediately handed a gin and tonic. "My wife knows what I like." He cheers and takes a sip. Becca always informs the staff to keep Dan's drinks coming. He usually takes the next day off if he has to work.

With a smile, I order Knob Creek and another flute. Mike makes an impressed look. "The boys came out to party tonight." He orders gin and tonic too. We raise our glasses in a circle and drink deeply.

"So you brought a date this year?" Dan is leaning on the bar looking at me intently.

"What the?...Mike just asked the same thing. I *have* brought a girl here before, ya know." I try to avoid more of his questions. *I had enough of that already.*

They answer in unison, "No you haven't," and laugh.

I roll my eyes and raise my palms up, shrugging. "I've brought lots of girls around."

Becca comes up to us, putting her hand on Dan's back and mine at the same time. "So you brought Lucy...is it serious?" Mike and Dan start laughing before I can even say anything. Becca just looks between all of us.

"I think he's in looove." Mike makes a puckering noise. I smack his head.

Becca answers seriously though, "It's about time." I smile at her, she's the mother hen to Dan's big brother routine.

Dan just keeps looking at me. I shake my head and Mike and I head back into the living room.

We find a guy I don't know standing over Lucy and Stephie. He's right in front of Lucy, though. She has a half-full flute in her hand again, too.

She's laughing as I walk up to the guy. I don't say anything, just take in what's happening. The guy is obviously looking down her dress and standing too close, his own flute empty. She's leaning back, but laughing loudly, tits shaking too much, taking a sip of champagne. I have to calm my instant reaction, taking a breath before taking the step into her view.

She sees me and a look of confusion crosses her face. She's reacting to the steely look I can feel, my jaw clenched, lips pressed into a tight line. "Hey..." She sees the glasses in my hand, Mike standing behind me, and she freezes in mid-greeting. Stephie just looks at Mike with a hand out for her gin and tonic, a small smile on her face.

I imagine for a second what I would like to do in this situation, if Lucy and I were further along in our relationship. I take a deep breath and try to calm myself, my fingers squeezing both flutes. *Good thing Becca insists on good glasses or I might need stitches tonight.* I allow a grin to cross my features.

As Lucy falters, the guy turns in my direction. Mike immediately steps in between us. "Hey, we haven't met. I'm Dan's old college buddy, Mike. This is Max." He remains between us. The guy smiles slightly and takes in the two glasses in my hands. He figures out that Lucy is with me and he quickly takes a step back. He's probably also reacting to my hard look and tensed arms.

"I work with Dan in publishing." He quickly puts out his hand for Mike to shake, then for me. I just shrug sarcastically with the two glasses still in my hands. Stephie jumps up to stand next to Mike, with a quick glance at me and eyes wider for a second, a smirk on her lips. I move past him and look at Lucy.

She has the most perfect look of guilt and shame, like I caught her in the act of misbehaving. I have to stop myself from smiling. *I want to keep that look on her face as long as I can.* She looks down at the glass in her hand already and then back up at me. She tries to smile, but only gets to a small one before stopping again.

I hand her the glass of wine I'm holding and she takes it with a small, "Thanks," now holding two glasses, looking embarrassed again.

I lean over her slowly and put my hand on the other glass, with an edge to my voice and a wink, "I'll take this for you." I pull it out of her hand violently quick, the liquid swishing, but not leaving the glass, the base of the flute hitting her fingers. She just looks up at me with the perfect cocktail of emotions, a heaping amount of shame with a splash of fear. I sit next to her and put my hand high on her thigh.

I ignore the guy as he quickly walks away; as Mike pulls Stephie away too, she gives us one last look over her shoulder.

I decide not to say something about Lucy's behavior. *We're not there yet. Not the right time to reveal that much of myself and certainly not around a bunch of other people.* Lucy is rubbing her fingers against the coolness of the glass I gave her. I take her hand and kiss her palm. Her fingers are a little red where the flute hit them, but she relaxes somewhat.

"Is that bourbon in your hand, mister?" She's leaning over me now, looking at the drink I'm holding.

"Yes." I'd forgotten all about teasing her with it. "Knob Creek actually...I believe you're familiar with it." I'm grinning at her now.

She hits my chest and leans over me. I notice her glass is nearly empty again. "Give me that." She reaches for the glass, but I just leave it on the arm of the sofa, out of her reach, pushing her shoulder back with my hand.

"Nope...told you. Not a little girl's drink." Our faces are close together, her upper body now fully leaning on me, only my hand keeping any distance between us. Her laughter dies down in response to the look on my face though. I'd meant to only tease her and let her have a sip, but my anger from earlier makes my look harder than I intended.

She starts to move back and say something, but I pull her towards me and kiss her. She responds by pushing into me more and kissing back harder.

"Get a room." Dan is standing over us. Lucy blushes and hides her face behind her hair, turning towards me, smiling.

Stephie walks over with Becca, "Come on, Lucy, the tour's starting."

Lucy laughs and gets up without saying anything else. I watch her walk away, the sway of her ass under the thin material of her dress making the outline of her thong clearly visible.

I stand up next to Dan now, taking a big gulp. "So, what did Becca get you this year?" He raises his brows up and down wickedly.

"I had a really nice time." Her words are slurred. I'm keeping her up as much as holding her as we walk down her street.

"I can tell." I laugh as she nearly trips on the sidewalk and I have to pull her upright again.

We make it up her stairs and I find her key in her purse. She is trying for a seductive look, but only manages a sloppy grin, "Are you going to come in this time?"

"Yes." I push the door open and lead her inside.

"Oh, goody." She laughs a hiccup and leans into me more. I keep one hand on her to keep her from falling as she ping-pongs around her living room in an effort to kick off her shoes. Suddenly she is pushing herself against me again, "Wanna carry me to bed and have your way with me?"

My cock stiffens instantly at this thought. I pick her up and carry her over to her bed, she yells out, "Oh, goody!" again.

I stand her up, keeping her in one arm against me and pulling her covers back with the other. I get her to lie down and pull the covers over her. Her arms are pulling me down around my neck. "No...Get in bed...Please?" Her little girl voice is almost too much to resist; but I don't want our first time to be like this, with her drunk and unable to decide for herself. She nearly kills me when she says, "I want you to tell me what to do...to *control* me like you like to do. You do like to be in control don't you?"

"Get some sleep, little girl." I go to kiss her forehead, but she turns her head up and I give in to kissing her deeply, pulling her up to a seated position.

"I am your little girl, aren't I?" Her eyes are sparkling, her lips wet, a smile playing across them. Her hand tries to reach into my pants. I pull her hand away gently and hold both of them in mine. She pouts, "I thought you wanted me."

"I do."

"Then take me." She falls back against her pillow, her tits bouncing. She opens her eyes when I don't move towards her, just keep her hands in mine, watching her. "I'll do whatever you want, Max...whatever you command. I like that you're old fashioned...controlling..."

I have to hold my breath to calm myself before standing up. I lean over her again and kiss her forehead one last time as her eyes fight to stay open.

"Tomorrow, little girl."

14 Her

Slowly opening my eyes, I'm a little disoriented for a second. I'm in my own bed, it's still dark. *So it must be early*? As I roll over to see the time on my nightstand, my dress twists around my legs more. *I went to bed in my clothes*?

In an instant, I recall Max leading me into my apartment and getting me in bed. I cover my forehead with my hand. *Oh, God...Is he still here? No.* I don't hear anyone else around. I vaguely remember him kissing me before I fell completely asleep.

It's only 4:00 a.m., the clock greenly illuminates a bottle of water and two aspirins on my nightstand. *How sweet of him to think to do that.* I down half the bottle in one gulp, getting out of bed. I pad into the bathroom, change into a tank top and sweatshorts hanging on the door.

As my head melts the pillow into shape, I fall back asleep wishing for Max in bed with me.

I'm bolted awake. The dog upstairs is barking, louder with each knock on my door. It's 10:00 a.m. now. Rushing to the door, I can't see who it is. *Max must have closed my blinds last night too.*

I see him smiling at me through the peephole. I open the door a little and he walks right in, trailing the most wonderful coffee smell behind him.

"Good morning, sleepy," he kisses my head. *God, I didn't even look at myself before I opened the door.* I stop in front of a mirror, wiping my raccoon eyes and pushing my bedhead hair down and back into a knotted ponytail. He sets down two cups and two bags on my coffee table. "I figured you might need some coffee this morning." His smile is sweet, but his expression is a little chastening.

"Yeah...sorry about that. I didn't realize how much I had until we were walking home," I take the coffee he hands me. "Thank you. ...And thanks for being such a gentleman last night too," I say quietly into my cup.

"No problem. I think my friends were a little to blame too." He nods his head towards the bags. "There's milk and sugar in there if you like. And I wasn't sure if you like sweet or savory in the morning, so there's chocolate croissants or bagels and cream cheese." My stomach actually growls at the mention of food.

"My hero! I like my bagels toasted, how bout you?" As I head into the kitchen with the bag of food, already eating a croissant.

"Toasted is great, thanks."

"What's in the other bag?" I ask upon returning with knives and plates of toasted goodness.

"A new deadbolt. I'm going to install it for you." He pulls a large plastic package out to show me.

"You don't have to do that."

"Yes, I do. It's not safe for you to have a door to the street and only a tiny lock." He pulls some tools out of the other plastic bag. "Your safety is important to me." He returns to the sofa and kisses me as he sits back down to eat his bagel.

"Well...thank you. I'll have to tell my landlord."

"There's an extra key you can give your landlord too. See I thought of everything." He gives a very self-satisfied smile with this.

"And humble too," I pat and push his shoulder a little.

After finishing our bagels, I continue eating the rest of the croissant while Max starts on the lock. My cell phone starts ringing by my bed. I jump up with a guilty look towards Max, but he ignores this.

Billy calling. Shit. I totally forgot about our plans for today. It's 10:30, we're supposed to be meeting in an half hour.

"Hey, Lucy. It's Billy. How are ya?"

"Um...great. Uh...I know we had plans to meet today..." I walk into my kitchen, so Max won't overhear me.

"Yeah. I was thinking by the parking lot entrance near the old boat building."

"Um...I'm sorta feeling under the weather today... Can I get a raincheck?" I feel awful lying to him, but I can't very well leave with Max here.

"Oh...yeah. No problem. I'll give ya a call later this week."

"Thank you."

"Feel better, Luce. And text me if you need anything. I can always stop by with some soup?"

"That's sweet. I'll be fine. Thanks, again, Billy."
Hanging up, I don't want to go right back into the living room yet in case Max heard any of that. I head into the bathroom instead, brush my teeth, wash my face and add a little makeup. I also think about last night some more.

I keep replaying what I said to Max and how he responded. I know I was drunk, but I've never been so direct with a guy before. *Probably because I've never had a guy be so direct with me before.*

I had a boyfriend once who liked to role-play in college. He would order me around and have me strip-tease for him, but he wasn't like that all the time and he certainly wasn't like that outside of sex.

Max is different. He likes to be in control all the time and last night I confessed to liking it that way. I'm blushing again thinking this.

...and we haven't even made out yet!

I'm still laughing at myself as I quietly return to the living room. Max is almost finished with the door. He proudly shows off my new and improved safety. "Thank you, again."

He wraps his arms around my waist. "Gotta take care of my girl." I smile at his use of that phrase again. "Get dressed and let's go for a walk."

Now that I blew off my plans with Billy, I might as well enjoy the day with Max. "Okay. Be right back." I quickly change into cutoff shorts and a clingy t-shirt.

15 Him

The park is full of kids, parents, and couples like us. The ducks and geese are vying for an old man's bread. Lucy's laughter matches the kids' and doesn't fail to make me smile even more. "This is one of my favorite spots in the city."

"Mine too." As she squeezes my upper arm again.

I walk us towards a park bench a little way from the water and pull her onto my lap. I barely feel her weight on my legs, but adjust so the response of my cock isn't so obvious. I brush her hair away from her neck and kiss lightly from her earlobe down to her shoulder. I feel the goosebumps on her arms, her nipples standing out, as she turns her face towards mine for a deeper kiss. My hands explore her back, thighs, neck. We start to get some stares from the uptight moms and older women.

"Maybe we should keep walking," Lucy says shyly looking around and getting up.

"Are you hungry? There's good Thai near my place."

"I can't believe I'm saying this after all those carbs this morning...but I'm actually hungry. Thai sounds yummy."

I hail a cab. "I thought you hated cabs." She pokes my ribs.

"Gotta give Jeff a day off sometime."

"Let me guess...you want to do the ordering?" She's poking my ribs again, but smiling at least. The restaurant is just thinning out from the lunch crowd, so we have a corner of the place to ourselves.

I grab her chair seat and yank her closer to me, "Of course." I take the menu out of her hand and set it down on the table. She doesn't protest and I smile. "What's your favorite kind of curry?"

"Green, please."

"Excellent choice." I fight back a wider smile remembering this as one of the biggest problems with Natalie. She took offense that I always ordered for her. *But, then again, I didn't start out the right way with her. Hopefully, I am with Lucy. By what she said last night, I am.*

She just smiles while I give our order to the waitress. "I love Tom Yum Gai." She squeezes my arm with both hands. "So what's with the old school you ordering everything, anyway?"

I'd hoped to avoid this conversation for a little longer, so I give a half answer. "It's how I was raised. My dad...well, he's actually my stepdad really...he was very old fashioned and strict. He took really great care of my mom, me, and my little brother. Taught me everything I know about being a good man."

"Was your dad around too?" Her hand hasn't left my arm, the warmth trailing her fingers up and down.

"No. He ended up leaving when I was just a kid. I think he did some merchant marine shit in Alaska for a while. My stepdad, Ron Traeger, actually adopted us when he married my mom. And I never heard from my deadbeat dad again."

"That sucks. I'm sorry you had to go through that." Her voice is so soft and sweet, I can imagine hearing it in bed.

"It wasn't so bad. Ron's been a good dad to us. He really helped my mom be a better person too." *I'm not ready to get into that just yet.* "How bout you? Mom and Dad? Siblings?"

"My folks are still married. They're visiting me tomorrow actually. They live in Arizona now and are coming through on a trip. I have an older brother. He's married and lives here with their two kids. My nieces are adorable."

"Are you close with your family?"

"Not really....I mean...well, we get along fine, but I don't see them often. I see my parents once or twice a year, my brother about the same. I usually go up to his place for holidays. PJ's 15 years older than me, so we weren't really raised together. How old is your brother?" She seems uncomfortable talking about her family and quick to change the subject back to mine.

"My brother, Jake, is 32. He lives with his girlfriend in Old Town. We hang out a lot, but he went down a different path than our dad wanted for us. We were both supposed to be lawyers and take over the family firm. Jake dropped out of law school. He's still finding himself I think."

"Ah...family pressure. That's something I know all too well." Her whole body has tensed up, shoulders raised, hands between her legs now.

"What kind of pressure does your family put on you?" I take her hand and place it on my leg instead, putting my hand back on her thigh, not letting the physical connection with her go.

"My folks think I should be married and barefoot by now. I mean, they *are* proud of me. My dad just doesn't like that I live alone in a big city...I think they worry more about me since they've moved away." She keeps her hand on my leg, but remains tense.

"Sounds like good family values to me." *Good sign, she doesn't move her hand away*. "If I had a sister, I wouldn't want her living alone in this city."

"I had roommates in college and I hated dealing with their shit all the time. I like being on my own...for now anyway."

I touch her nose lightly, "You should watch your language, young lady." *I'm pressing my luck*.

She just laughs, "Yeah, I talk like a sailor sometimes. Drives my mom crazy. She thinks it's because I hang out with Tracy, who really is an artist with words." She laughs again. I decide not to say more for now.

She changes the subject, "Do you like working for your dad?"

"I only work for him when he needs something. For the most part, I have my own clients and dealings with the LPE Group and some other developers." We're both sipping and blowing on our soup, but I keep my hand on her the whole time.

"Do you like being a lawyer, the kind of work you do?"

"Yeah. I do. It's interesting and each project, each client is a little different. Keeps me busy."

"Well...I told you I'm in Human Resources..." She is looking at me more than eating now. I know she wants me to ask her about what she does. I only smile.

Natalie had been such a pain in the ass about her job. Always using it as an excuse to put distance between us. I don't want to encourage Lucy to do the same. *I don't really care what she does now...it's more what she's willing to do later that matters to me.* I grin thinking about this, raising one eyebrow. *I still can't believe I'm already this far gone for this girl.*

She smiles questioningly back at me, but continues talking, "...I do recruiting for an accounting firm. I mostly fill the non-accounting jobs though, like marketing and."

I interrupt her. "You must have good instincts when it comes to people." She smiles at this and doesn't look offended that I stopped her from saying more. *Good.*

"I think I do..." She takes a bite again. "I like to believe that I can get to the heart of a person pretty quickly and judge a good fit."

I take her hand and place it on my chest, "How bout my heart?"

"It's beating pretty fast." She blushes and starts to pull away, but I keep her hand there.

"No. What do you think of our fit?" I continue to look her directly in the eye.

Her blushing increases, she breaks the stare and looks down, but I wait for her to look back up again with a smile changing back and forth from big to small. "I like you..."

"I like you too, Lucy." I kiss her, tasting the chili sauce from her last bite.

We walk slowly down my street. In front of my building, I stop. "This is my place."

She looks straight up the high-rise and back down into the lobby. "Nice. What floor are you on?"

I open the glass door for her, "The top."

She purses her lips, "Of course." She giggles. We walk past the doorman, who waves at me.

I press my keycard against the elevator lock and the doors open. "Is this a private elevator?"

"Sort of. It's for the top floor condos only. There's four of us." I can see that she's trying to hide being impressed. "With one of my real estate deals, I was able to buy into this building while it was still in the development stage."

"Wow. Very impressive. I thought finding a one-bedroom in Lincoln Park was hard enough."

"I like your place. It's very sweet and warm. Like you." I squeeze her waist to my side as the elevator opens again. I keep us walking this closely all the way to my door.

I open and let her enter first. I know my place is impressive and I want to see her reaction for the first time. Mike always jokes about how much pussy I must get with this address. But he knows that I don't let many people up here. I like my privacy.

The entry hallway is all white, with a long table and tall mirror behind it. I take her purse and set it on the bench under the table. She continues walking in without saying a word, just looking around with her mouth wide open. I stop walking behind her, enjoying my view too.

Finally, she turns to me at the end of the hall where it opens up to the main living room, "Wow. This place is great."

"Thanks. I hired a decorator, so I can't take credit for everything in here, but I do love it." I catch up with her in the long living/dining room combo. The floor to ceiling windows highlight the surrounding cityscape. I lead her out to my terrace for a better view.

Standing with my arms around her, I press her legs against the low wall, burying my face in her hair. "This is such a great view of the city. Is this patio just yours or do you share it with the other apartments?"

"Just mine." I press myself a little more into her lower back, giving in to the urgency her curves create. She presses back slightly, but then freezes, a little uncertain of what she's doing. Her hesitancy only makes me harder.

I turn her around to face me, her mouth awaiting mine, lips wet and soft. My hands travel from her hips up to her tits, using just my thumbs to whisper across her erect nipples. Her gasp is quick and soft inside my mouth.

I pull her shirt up over her head before she can stop me. Her eyes dart around, but I silence her protests, "No one can see us." My kiss is more firm; her response is more urgent. Her hands go to my waist, but again freeze, uncertain. I lower my kisses to the tops of her tits, pushing the lace bra aside to tease her nipples harder; her hands find a home in my hair, tugging nicely.

Taking her hand, I lead her back into the living room. Sitting on the sofa, I position her to stand between my legs, my hands on her hips. "Take off your bra."

She frowns and smiles, but says nothing, reaching behind her to unhook. She slowly lets the straps fall down her arms, keeping her hands over the front. I raise one brow and nod my head for her to continue.

She hesitates, but then quickly removes the bra, keeping her tits covered with her left arm. I move my hands to her ass, cupping both cheeks and squeezing hard, forcing her off balance. Her hands automatically go to my shoulders to stop from falling forward, her tits gently pendulum in front of my face. I slowly wrap my tongue around one then the other nipple, looking up into her eyes. She's biting her lower lip.

Lucy digs her fingers into my shoulders and slides onto my lap as I pull her down. Her thighs are tight against my sides. My arms cover her whole back, both hands in her hair. Pulling her head back gently, I nibble her neck, pressing her down.

"Push your hips against me," my voice is low and deep, more of a growl into her neck. She moves her hips, a rocking motion, her thighs pressing harder, back arching more.

I pick her up, her legs stay locked around me, and she buries her face in my neck. I carry her with my hands under her ass into my bedroom.

I stop next to the bed and stand her up, pushing her off me a little. "I want to see you. Take off your shorts."

She drops her hands from my shoulders, puts her tits out a little more. "You first."

I harden my look, but decide to let it slide...*this time*.

I unbutton my shirt and let it drop to the floor behind me. With two fingers, I grab the front of her shorts and pull her forwards, then quickly push her back, keeping her balanced with only my fingers. Her look of fear is all too fleeting, quickly changing to surprise then a smile. "Undress. Now." I keep my look hard but my voice quiet.

She hesitates again, looking down at my hand. I move it away. Not looking up, she slowly removes her shorts, letting them pool at her feet for a second before kicking them behind her. She's perfect, soft and full, strong and curved, a gift my eyes devour.

She still hasn't looked up, her hair covering her face more as it falls out of the loose knot. I close the step between us, push her purple thong down her hips and thighs. She leaves it at her feet. She lightly touches my chest, just her fingertips tracing the outline of my muscles. The heat of her kiss on the middle of my chest sends a charge down my stomach. My cock twitches.

I walk her backwards to the edge of my bed. She's staring up at me now. The blue of her eyes brightens. I undo my belt, taking my shorts and boxers off together. They fall heavily to the floor. With my arm bracing her back, I kneel down onto her, laying us flat against each other.

I have to hold myself up not to crush her. Her hands are digging into my arms. I push her legs open with mine, her low moan muffled in my chest. My right hand opens her pussy, middle finger barely entering, her heat wet against my palm. She moves her hips slightly to try to pull my finger in deeper. I press her clit down with the length of my finger. *Not yet*. She squirms but stops pressing.

I kiss her face, lips, neck, continuing to gently stroke her clit with only one finger, barely inside her. When I feel her pussy lips tighten, I don't want to wait any longer. Moving up, I force my hard cock inside her in one rough push. She lets out a high pitched moan.

I stay deep inside her, not moving, feeling her depth trying to take all of me, her hips pushing down into the bed, away from me. This feels like where I've always belonged.

"No. Stay still." She stops moving, her fingers digging into my back, nails scraping. I push harder into her. "Does that hurt?"

"No," it's barely a breath out of her, "a little."

"Squeeze me." Her eyes pop open at this. I grin at her. "Go on."

She closes her eyes again and gently bites my chest as her pussy firms around my cock. "Good girl." I pull out quickly and push in again harder. Her moan is louder, her head thrown back against the pillow. I thrust several times just as hard, my breathing matching hers.

Slowing down again, I feel her hips grinding into mine, trying to push me faster. "I said stay still." I stop thrusting with my cock just inside her lips. Her eyes pop open. Her look almost makes me come...surprise, fear...and shame. I grab her hands and hold them down above her head, still not re-entering her.

"Can you stay still for me, Lucy?" I kiss her nose. I'm holding back as long as I can.

"Yes...yes," her answer is more a plea, a moan. I enter her hard, her breath catches her scream, turning it into a strangled moan. My body slaps hers faster in complete abandon, a need rising with our moans. We climax together, as I collapse on top of her.

It takes a while for our breathing to even out, staying in rhythm. I slide off to her side, keeping my arm draped across her stomach, hand caressing her tit gently. She slowly opens her eyes.

16 Her

My pussy is still pulsing under the weight of him. When he moves off, the air feels too cool and I can feel my nipples hardening, his touch helping.

I still can't believe I'm in bed with him. It's been over eight months since my last time, as Tracy keeps reminding me. *Well, she won't worry about me re-virginizing now.* I press my legs together. *Hell, I'm actually sore.*

I open my eyes and am surprised to see it's still light out. *Who has first-time mind-blowing sex in the middle of the day?* I turn my head towards him and return his smile.

His teeth are so perfect, his lips a deeper shade of red now, his forehead still glistening from sex. I could stare into his eyes all day. *Oh, God...I think I'm having dreamy love thoughts already.*

"Are you thirsty?" He moves to get out of bed. His back muscles stretch and tense, his arms popping out in detail. I pull the sheet up to cover myself.

"Yes, please." I can't look away as he stands, his ass two perfectly hard cantaloupes, his legs lean and lightly covered in soft brown hair. I blush seeing nail marks on one of his shoulders.

He walks around the bed and picks up his boxers. I look down so he doesn't catch me staring. He goes over to a tall dresser and takes out two t-shirts. He puts one on and tosses the other onto the bed at my feet. "Put this on."

I sit up after he leaves the room. Getting out of bed, I pull the t-shirt over my head appreciating that it reaches to my knees. I also retrieve my undies from the floor and head into the attached bathroom.

This place is amazing. The bathroom is a sea of marble, floor, walls, counters, a shower stall the size of my whole bathroom, a tub I could swim in. I find the toilet behind its own door. *Yep, I am definitely sore...and my face is going to hurt if I don't stop smiling.*

He didn't come back into the bedroom, so I slowly walk out into the hallway. I can hear him moving around and follow the noise around the corner. His kitchen looks out into the open dining and living room, an all-black and stainless steel place. He's opening a bottle of champagne as I enter. The pop startles me and I laugh.

"We're celebrating. Grab those glasses." He points to a countertop and I follow him out to the sofa with two flutes.

Tucking my legs under myself, covering my knees with his shirt, I lift a glass for him to pour. "You are so beautiful." He wetly kisses my mouth, handing the glass back.

I've always hated how easily I blush. "Thank you."

From the hallway, I can hear my phone ringing, the tone getting louder. I jump up and race over to my purse, thinking it might be my parents. I answer without looking at the callerid.

"Hello."

"Hey!" It's Tracy. "How was your big date with Billy the Bullet? Was he faster than...a speeding bullet?" She's laughing at her own joke. *Oh, God. I have her on speaker*. I quickly switch this off.

"Um...Trace...I'm going to have to call you back later." I turn towards the mirror. I'm beet red now. I turn quickly away.

"Oh, is he there? Am I interrupting? I want details later!"

"Yeah...Okay...I'll call you when I'm home."

"You slut. I'm proud of you." She laughs before hanging up.

Setting my phone down, I wait before walking back into the living room. Max isn't sitting on the sofa anymore. I look around and see him standing on the patio again. *Maybe he didn't hear that?* I can hope.

Picking up the other glass of champagne, I walk out there. "Sorry about that. I thought it might be my folks. They're driving in and said they might arrive early."

"But it wasn't your parents." My heart drops for a second. *So he did hear*. His look is distant and dark, brows shading his light eyes, his voice harsher.

"No...That was Tracy." I feel warm and red all over suddenly.

"I gathered that." He takes a slow sip of wine, not taking his eyes off of me. "So who's Billy? The guy who called earlier?"

I take a sip and swallow loudly. "Um...Yeah. I had plans for a bike ride today..." I'm not really sure what to say after that.

"Is he someone you're seeing?" His voice is so low and steady, it's almost hypnotic.

"Um...not really. I just met him...friend of a friend sorta thing..." I'm really uncomfortable now, I drop his gaze and take another sip, turning towards the view.

He stands behind me like earlier, pressing me into the low wall. He pulls me towards him with his arm around my chest, holding my left shoulder. I can feel his heart beating against my back. "I know this may be too soon to have this conversation, Lucy." He takes a deep breath, my body moving with his. "But I want you to know that you're special. I haven't felt this in a long time...how I feel about you. I think we could have something very special if you're willing to give it a chance."

I'm floored. Speechless. He is definitely more direct than any other guy I've ever known. I turn around to face him and am surprised at how stern his face looks, jaw set, eyes piercing. "I really like you too, Max." It sounds so lame, but I'm uncertain of saying anything else. That feeling in my stomach has returned...the lust.

He lifts my chin with one finger up to him. "I want you all to myself."

I just blink in response, unable to think. *We did just sleep together...but, we hardly know each other.* "You hardly know me."

"And I want the chance for us to get to know each other without...distractions." His finger continues holding my head up.

"You aren't seeing other women?" I try for an accusatory tone, but fall short. I can hear the hope in my voice.

"Not since I met you."

"Well...you made it sound like you date around a lot."

He takes my hand and leads me over to a u-shaped sectional in the middle of the terrace. He pulls me onto his lap. His left arm rests behind me, his right hand goes under my shirt and holds my hip. The intimacy of his touch and this conversation continue to make me squirm.

His fingers squeeze into my hip a little more. "My last serious relationship was about five years ago. I have dated a lot of women since then." He pauses to smile, to take the sting out of his words. "But I haven't truly cared about anyone. A date was just a woman to take to an event or spend a little time with. No one that I've truly been myself with. Does that make sense to you?"

"Yes..."

"And I see in you someone I want to spend a lot of time with. That I want to be myself with you." He says this like it holds a different meaning for him, a significance I'm not getting. His eyes stare for an answer in mine.

"What do you mean...be yourself? How are you different with me?" I brush a wave away from his eyes, staring into the stark green.

"I have certain...beliefs...in how it should be between us." The confused look on my face must have been enough for him to continue trying to explain. "I want more from you, so I'm willing to put in more effort to have you. That's how it's different with you...for me."

"I...I really like you, too, Max." I falter in trying to match his honesty. "And I haven't been this excited about a guy in a long time too. My last real boyfriend was two years ago, so I don't jump into relationships...or bed...with just anyone." I finish with a small laugh, trying to lighten our talk.

"Good. I don't think you'll believe this, but I do know you, Lucy. I believe I know the real you...the one you may hide from others, but not from me. The one you showed me last night."

I blush at this. S*o he does remember everything I said too.* "So...what? After only a couple of dates, you want to be exclusively seeing each other?" *This whole conversation seems surreal. Isn't it usually the girl who pushes for commitment?*

"Yes." I wait for him to say more, but he just keeps holding my gaze.

"Oh." I have no idea what to say.

"Stop thinking so much and just tell me how you feel." His crooked grin is in place again. My back relaxes at seeing this.

"I'd like to see where this goes with us, too."

"Good." He lightly slaps the side of my butt and hip. "Then it's settled. No more friends of friends, sorta seeing other guys."

"...And no meaningless dates with other girls for you?" I poke his chest.

He pulls me into a kiss in answer. His hand moves up to my nipple, giving it a tweak, then pressing with his thumb. I can feel his cock hardening at my side. I squirm against him and move so I can put my hand between us. Through his boxers, I rub the top of his cock, eliciting a moan from us both.

He startles me by picking me up and heading inside. I feel very light in his arms, his broad shoulders anchors for me to hold onto. He tickles my side, making me laugh and move around, but he doesn't drop me.

Just as we're entering his bedroom, my phone rings from the hallway. He puts me down quickly and turns before I can get through the doorway. He looks at the callerid before handing me the phone, "You're lucky…it's your mom." His look is unreadable as he walks back into his bedroom, but my stomach responds to him again.

"Hi, Mom." I'm distracted thinking about what Max meant by lucky. Mom is going on about their trip so far, and how they'll be at my place for dinner. "Okay, great. There's some nice places around me that I think Dad will like."

I hang up and decide to turn my phone off.

17 Him

I head into the bathroom and start a shower. Bracing my arms on the counter, I stare closely at myself in the mirror. *I need to slow down.* But every part of me wants to push forward. *Maybe it's better this way.* I waited months before talking to Natalie about my expectations and that definitely didn't go over well then. Girlfriends before Nat didn't work out any better. I wasn't sure about what I wanted enough to be clear with them.

But with Lucy, I want to have a very sure start, to be clear on what we have together. *So no matter how much I fear pushing her away, I need to be true to myself on what I want, what I demand.* I grin at this. She's already shown a readiness to please, to listen, an attentiveness. Last night she was hard to leave. *I just need to see how far she's willing to go when she's thinking clearly.*

I can hear her in the bedroom again. I step into the doorway, "Come here." Watching her walk towards me, I'm on my way to hard again. One foot in front of the other like a dancer, her arms crossed in front pushing the shirt up to reveal more of her tanned and toned legs, tits perky sitting on her arms. But it's the look on her face that has my cock hard. A blending of desire, uncertainty, and shyness.

I put my arms around her, crossing at her back. "So are your folks in town already?"

She puts her arms around me too. "Not yet. They'll be here for an early dinner though. I should probably get going. Need to clean my place more before my mom gets here and starts doing it herself."

"You need to get cleaned up too...I could help with that." I pull her towards the bathroom, where the shower is steaming behind glass doors.

"Well...I do need to shower today..." She smiles and I let go of her. I pull her shirt over her head and follow with mine. She waits till I drop my boxers before removing her thong. I lead her into the shower, blinded for a second by the steam.

She moves to the back wall; I press a button and several sprayers turn on. She laughs as we're pelted with warm water from all angles, her hands up, pushing the water away. I press another button, and the water is directed through two rain heads in the ceiling. I'm under one; she's under another.

I signal with my index finger for her to come to me. She slowly moves into focus in the steam, legs scissoring one in front of the other again. Standing under the rain head, the water cascades over her, flattening her curls against her head, shoulders, chest; her tits are shining, nipples perky. I kiss her mouth; water rivers between us, I push it away with my tongue as it fills even the small spaces between our lips.

Reaching down, my hand follows the contour of her stomach and soft hairy mound to her pussy. Her legs spread for me quickly, wanting. I look at her; she has her eyes closed, head leaning back slightly, forehead in the water, arms clutching my shoulders to her. Her mouth opens willingly for my tongue. I kiss her hard, pushing my fingers into her harder, crushing her clit. Her gasps take in a little water, but I don't stop for her small coughs. She's gasping again with my fingers in and out, pressing deep inside her.

I pull my fingers away, and she lets out a pleading little moan, wanting more, fingers digging into me. Her eyes open.

I shove her hard against the tiled wall, away from the water now. She gasps, but her arms are up for my embrace, pressing against her tits, leaving tile indentations in her back and ass.

I lift her quickly, rubbing her raw against the shower, her arms clutching around my head, her legs snaking around my middle. My cock finds her pussy and stops with just the head inside.

She bucks against me, trying to get more of me in.

I wait till she stops moving, before shoving deep inside her. Her screaming moan is right next to my ear, the water muffles the volume, but not the pain mixed with pleasure.

"You want more?" I stay deeply pressed inside her, pinning her against the tile, water running down my back.

She digs her fingernails into my shoulders, the hot water stinging now. "Yes. Please!" She emits a moan, a plea, an animal growl to match my own.

Holding her against the tile, I fuck her hard. My cock slams up into her, my knees shaking when we finally come together, her head smashed next to mine, arms squeezing my neck, my fingers digging into every inch of her I can reach.

I wait until her arms loosen before letting her legs down. She sways a little, and pushes aside her hair plastered by water to her forehead. "I think I'm dizzy."

"You're welcome." I laugh as she slaps my one shoulder, but I don't let Lucy go until I'm sure she can stand alone.

I grab a bar of soap and suds up my chest and underarms, watching her watch me. I pass her the soap and look on as she does the same, passing it back to me. We take turns washing, until I turn her around and rub her back with warm sudsy water, feeling the contour of her muscles, tensing and relaxing with my massage. Her moan is soft and long.

I hand her the soap and turn around, she runs her hands up and down my back, even lightly going over my ass before applying pressure to my sore shoulder muscles. I moan too.

I turn around, "Hand me the shampoo." She reaches and puts some in her hand, then glides the goop over my fingers. "Turn around again." I put my soapy fingers in her hair and massage, pull, and rub her head into a sudsy ball. "I love your hair."

She laughs, an echo in the enclosed space only slightly softened by the water. "I hope you have conditioner too. Otherwise you're gonna have to love frizz."

I slap her butt lightly. "Conditioners over there," I point over her shoulder to another bottle. She does the same, rubbing a small amount off onto my fingers, and stays facing me. I finger comb this through her tangled mop. The action pulls her face backwards for me to see more, causing her to frown and groan in pain slightly. I kiss her lips each time her head is thrown back. She responds each time, her fingers still loosely around my waist, tongue darting around mine, eyes half closed. *Damn...she's beautiful*

"I want to meet your parents."

"Hmm...Not sure that's such a good idea..." She hesitates at the door, still scrunching her hair dry with her fingers. "My folks are only in town for a day or two. I don't know if I can spring a new guy on them just like that."

"I'm not just *a* guy, Lucy. And since your parents don't live around here, I'd like them to meet me. Wouldn't you?" This is a perfect opportunity to push her a little.

"Um...well..... How bout I tell them about you tonight over dinner and you can meet us for breakfast tomorrow?"

"Perfect." I open the door and take the elevator down with her, holding her close the whole time. "I called Jeff to give you a ride home."

"I thought it was his day off?"

"He doesn't mind the extra hours." She reaches for the door and I push her hand away. "A lady lets a gentleman open doors for her."

"You *are* old fashioned." She laughs. "Thank you."

Our kiss lingers as Jeff waits by the car door. "Thank you for such a nice day." She's almost whispering even though no one is near.

"Thank you." Our one last kiss is one to remember. "Call me after dinner tonight. I want to make sure you are home safe." She kisses my nose and says she'll call. *That's my good girl.*

18 Her

Dad is walking around looking at my windows, while Mom has disappeared into my bathroom. *Probably snooping.* "I still don't like the idea of you being right on the street like this. Anyone could get in these windows." He's pointing to the front ones off the porch.

"The windows are safe, Dad. Besides my neighbor's dog would let me know if anyone was walking around here. Butch barks at everyone."

He doesn't look convinced. "At least there's a good lock on the door."

I've been nervous about bringing up Max, but this seems like a prime time. I almost mumble, "Max put that on for me."

Behind me, Mom asks, "Who's Max, honey?"

"He's a guy I'm seeing..." She smiles bigger. *Of course she's happy to finally hear about a guy in my life again.*

"Actually, I'm hoping you won't mind if he joins us for breakfast tomorrow?"

"Of course not." Her smile cannot get any bigger. "How long have you two been dating?"

I sidestep this question. "Only for a little while, but I think you'll like him."

"Does he have a job?" *Subtle, Dad.*

"He's a lawyer." *So there.*

"Hmm..." As close as he can get to approving.

"Well, if you like him, I'm sure we'll like him, honey." Mom hugs me. *Yeah...like that's always been true.*

"Hey."

"How was dinner?"

"Good. I took my parents to a pizza place near here. I think they liked it." I'm in bed already, with the lights off. His husky and deep voice sounds even better in the dark. I can imagine him lying next to me, with his mouth on my ear. I ache still from our time together.

"Did you tell them about me?"

"Yes. I think you scored points with my dad by adding that lock to my door. And I told them you are joining us for breakfast."

"Good. I can't wait to meet them." He actually sounds excited about it. I've had to drag past boyfriends to family functions before. Max is new territory in so many ways.

"My brother might be there too...just so you're warned." *Let's see how he really feels about meeting my family.*

"Great." *Hmm...He may be too good to be true.* I suppress a giggle. "I'll pick you up and we can go together. What time?"

"10 o'clock. We're going to Eggceptional."

"Okay...I'll be there at 9:30. Get some sleep, baby." *Gee...my first nickname. He is too cute.*

"Good night, Max." I choke on a nickname for him.

"...Lucy?" I pause before hanging up.

"Yeah?"

"Wear a skirt tomorrow."

I pause before answering, my brows going up and down in the dark, "...sure." My stomach reacts with that tightening, flipping feeling again, a charge pulsing down to my pussy.

"Good night." He hangs up before I can say anything more.

19 Him

"Are you sure you want to meet everyone?" She paused in front of the door, looking into the restaurant.

I can just see an older couple and a guy inside waiting for a table. "Yes." I open the door.

"Hey, kiddo!" The guy comes over and hugs Lucy, before turning to me for a handshake. "I'm Paul."

"Max. Nice to meet you." Shaking his hand, I can see the family resemblance, same curly hair and blue eyes. I turn to the older couple who are standing on either side of Lucy now. Her mom is small like her, same eyes and hair. Her dad is staring me down.

"Mom, Dad, this is Max." She looks so nervous. I want to plant a kiss on her right there. I only smile.

"Max Traeger, Sir." I shake his hand firmly.

"Paul and Elizabeth." Her dad's shake is equally firm. Her mom's hand is delicate in mine, just like Lucy's.

As I turn towards the hostess stand, her mom says behind me, "We put our name in, but they say for a larger group it'll be a twenty to thirty minute wait."

I walk over to the stand and return with the hostess and menus. "Right this way." I direct her mom to follow the hostess. She raises her eyebrows and smiles at me.

"Bonus points with my dad. He hates to wait for food." Lucy pokes my ribs as she follows behind her brother. I watch her ass sway just visible in her tight cotton skirt under a long matching tunic tank.

We're seated at one end of an extra-large round table on the second floor of the restaurant. Pastries, coffee, and juices are brought over before we've even settled into our seats.

"We didn't order these, dear." Her mom is shooing the server away. He looks at me confused.

"It's all right, Elizabeth. I asked that they send over some starters for us. The cream puffs and muffins are the best here." Her dad is already buttering a muffin.

"Oh. Well... Thank you, Max." She looks much younger with a full smile, more like Lucy.

"Do you know someone here?" Her brother is looking around the room.

"This restaurant is part of a group that I partner." He nods his head in response, still looking around.

"I used to come here before we had kids. My wife and I lived around the block when we first got married." Paul Jr., is working on his second cream puff. "And these *are* the best. We would have to get here early to get a table though. Or wait in a long line and munch on these."

"Where are Cathy and the girls?" Lucy hasn't eaten anything, probably still too nervous. I squeeze her hand under the table. "My nieces are soooo cute." She informs me.

"Well. I wanted to wait till we were all together." PJ puts down his puff and takes hold of his mom's hand. "We're pregnant."

"Oh, son. That's great news." Paul Sr., grabs his other hand across the table, while Elizabeth is hugging him. "The best news!"

"Congratulations, PJ." Lucy gives him a hug and kiss too.

"Thanks. We're really excited. Cathy unfortunately is having a lot of morning sickness this time, so she wasn't up to making a trip downtown. And the girls were acting up this morning, so she figured it would be best to leave them at home. Besides, I know you'll want to see them. Cathy's hoping you'll come back to the house and stay tonight at least."

"That sounds like a good plan." Paul Sr., says through a mouthful of muffin. "We can stay an extra day or two for our grandkids."

Elizabeth is grinning even more and squeezes Paul's hand. "You know...I had a lot of morning sickness with you, PJ. Maybe it's a boy this time." But she keeps looking at Lucy, who in turn, avoids her stare, looking down at her plate mostly.

"That's what Cathy said too, Mom. We'll know in a few weeks. Luce...you wanna come over too, the girls would love to see you. There's a train that'll get you back into the city not too late."

"Yeah...I'd love to see everyone and see how Cathy is doing." Something in Lucy's response sounds sad though.

The waitress comes over for our orders and Lucy looks to me. I stop myself from kissing her right then. *Does she already understand that I'll order for her, no matter who's around?* Before she opens her mouth, I order pancakes and bacon for us both. "And I would like the fresh berries on top for the pancakes, not the pre-mixed in kind. Thanks."

"That sounds delicious. I'll have the same." Elizabeth closes her menu. Lucy smiles at me. She looks more relaxed now. No one noticed that she didn't even open her menu. *My good girl.*

Standing outside the restaurant, Lucy in my arms, I give her a small kiss, knowing she's uncomfortable with her parents and brother standing not too far away. "Call me when you get home tonight, baby."

"Will do." She kisses my cheek one more time. I walk her over to her waiting family.

"It was nice meeting you, Max." Elizabeth and Paul Sr., shake my hand again. "Hopefully, we'll see you again..." Her mom looks pointedly at Lucy, who rolls her eyes in response.

"You definitely will," I hug Lucy to my side a little.

"And thanks for the extra cream puffs. Cathy is going to love these." PJ holds up the cake box in his hands.

"No problem." I kiss the top of Lucy's head as a final goodbye.

As I walk away I can hear her mom saying, "He's such a gentleman. You should hold onto him..."

20 Her

This morning has been a nightmare. I over slept, my boss has been hell on heels, and this damn report keeps failing to save with my updates. *There is not enough coffee in the world to help right now.*

"Hey, stranger." I pull my hands away from my face and turn around. Tracy is standing in the doorway to my office.

"Hey." I know she's probably pissed at me for not calling her back this weekend. "Sorry I didn't call you. The weekend got *surprisingly* busy." I smile despite the bad day I'm having.

"I figured. Are you going to spill the details or do I have to torture them out of you?" She doesn't hold a grudge. It's one of the things I love most about her.

"How bout over lunch? I'm swamped and Cruela is riding her broom today."

"Okay. Meet downstairs at noon. I'll tell Laura." She gives me her coffee. "You look like you need this more than me today."

"You are a Goddess."

"So...How *was* your date with Billy?" Tracy is wasting no time. We only just ordered our sandwiches.

"Um...well...actually...I didn't make my date with Billy." I crinkle my nose and smile guiltily. She and Laura give me matching blank stares.

"What the fuck were you doing all weekend then?" Tracy slaps my shoulder. "Or should I say who the fuck?"

I just blush and press my lips together for a second before answering, "Max."

"Oh my God..." Laura is laughing.

"So wait. You spent the whole weekend with Max? What happened to Billy?" Tracy is wide-eyed and laughing too.

"Max came over early on Saturday, before Billy called. So I just cancelled. And one thing led to another..."

"You whore." Tracy is loud and a few people look at our table.

"Shhh..." I'm laughing though. I've been dying to tell them about Max. "I didn't spend the *whole* weekend with him. Remember, my folks were in town. But he did have breakfast with them yesterday."

"Wow. That's major. You introduced him to your parents?" Laura is leaning in, waiting for more details.

"And my brother. Max actually suggested it." I still can't believe how easy it was to have him there with my family. They couldn't stop talking later about what a great guy he was. Cathy was disappointed she didn't get to meet him.

"Why would he want to meet your family?" Tracy is looking skeptical.

"Well...because they don't live around here...so he just wanted to...to be friendly I think." I can't explain it to her. She hasn't even introduced Josh to hers and they live thirty minutes away.

"Well I think it's sweet." I can always count on Laura to be the romantic.

"I think it's weird." Tracy is devouring her sandwich and mumbles this around a biteful. "Did you have sex at least?"

"Tracy." Laura is slapping her now, laughing around a bite.

"Yes..." I'm shy about saying more.

"Thank God. At least you know it still works...hasn't closed shut on you." Tracy's laughing again.

"Oh...it works. Just fine thankyouverymuch." We're all laughing loudly now.

"So when are you going out with Billy the Bullet? Maybe you can make this a streak..." Tracy raises her eyebrows obnoxiously.

"Um...I don't think I'm going to go out with him..." I don't want to say why.

"Why not?" This time it's Laura's turn to grill me. "He's cute."

"Um...well...I want to see where this goes with Max..."

"So? There ain't no ring on your finger." Tracy is flipping me off with her ring finger. "And you don't have to get serious with the first guy you re-pop your cherry with."

"I know that…" I'm feeling defensive now.

"Do you like Max that much already?" Laura is watching me closely.

"Yes. I do." I want to put an end to this conversation. "And he likes me that much too. He even said so."

"Wow. A guy in touch with his feelings. Sure he's not gay?" Tracy is trying for a joke again, backing off.

"Definitely not gay." We're laughing more. "I think I'm still sore..." I whisper this knowing Tracy would get a kick out of it.

"Okay. Now I need more details! And we should have drinks. Let's go for happy hour tonight." Tracy is her usual loud self.

"Okay, but I'm meeting Max at 7:00." They exchange a look as we're getting up from the table, but don't say anything until we're outside.

"Tell him to join us," Tracy pushes my shoulder.

"We'd like to get to know him, too," Laura adds.

"Well, we have plans. But I can see if he can join us for Wednesday?"

"I think Billy might be there...Josh already invited him and Tad." Tracy's smile is more a grimace.

"Oh. Well." I feel a queasiness in my stomach at the thought of Max meeting Billy. "Then maybe you can meet him Friday instead."

"Friday is the Fourth party." Laura reminds me. "But we can get to know him at that."

Hmm...Not sure how I feel about introducing Max to a party full of people.

21 Him

I look at the time on my computer again. 10:17. She said she would be home early tonight. *Looks like I need to define early for her.*

My cell buzzes; the photo I took of her laughing in the park last weekend shows on the screen.

"Hey. Are you finally home?"

"Yes. I just walked in and wanted to call you right away." *She sounds tipsy.*

"It's later than I expected you to be." I'm trying to keep my voice even. We'd been out together the last two nights. Tonight though she said she had a weekly dinner with her girlfriends planned. I didn't like it, but I know that I can't push her on everything at once. *This next part could go badly and mess everything up.*

"Nooo...it's only...10:30 silly." She is definitely tipsy, her slurring is more pronounced.

"I expect you home by 9:30 if you're not with me." I hold my breath waiting for her response. I may be making a mistake doing this while she's drunk. *I've made this mistake before.*

"Is that a curfew?" She's laughing and sounding very cutesy, a hiccup interrupting her last word.

"Yes." I wait again.

"Well...I'm a big girl...and I can decide...for myself...what...time..." Her hiccups cut off the rest.

"You are *my* girl." I stress the word and pause. "And you'll behave yourself, even when I'm not with you to take care of you."

"Max, are you mad at me?" Her little girl voice is driving me crazy. My cock insistently stiffens.

"Get some sleep, Lucy. Call me at 12:00 tomorrow and we'll talk more." I hang up before she says anything else.

That went better than I'd hoped. But I'm going to have a hard time falling asleep now with this hard-on. I'm smiling though.

22 Her

My fuzzy head isn't the only thing making my stomach flip-flop today. I left the office early to avoid seeing Tracy and Laura before I could call Max. I feel guilty about last night.

Billy had been there and it was like a triple date. Tad and Laura ended up hooking up at the end of the night and Billy ended up sharing a cab with me. He kept trying to kiss me and I finally had to push him away and say I have a boyfriend to get him to stop. I don't think he believed me, but he didn't try anything more, just said, "You're a real tease," when I got out.

On the bright side, I know he didn't get the job. He'll get that happy news tomorrow.

Max finally answers my call, "Hi, Lucy. How are you feeling this morning?"

At least he can't see me blush over the phone. "I'm fine. Sorry I was so tipsy last night. Chianti just goes right to my head."

"You shouldn't have stayed out so late." I can hear traffic in the background. *He's probably in the car, with Jeff overhearing everything.* I blush more, embarrassed.

"Yeah, our Wednesday night thing always goes a little later than we plan..." I trail off, I don't want to talk more about last night. I don't want him to ask who was there. I realize that I wouldn't be able to lie to him if he did, because I care about him too much. But the calm anger in his voice is already making me a little nervous. *I'd be too afraid of how he'd react to answer him.* This revelation makes me swallow harder.

"I need to know you're safe. That means home, in bed, at a decent hour. And not out drunk with your friends."

I can't believe he's chastising me like this. But the guilt I feel about Billy being there last night makes me not say anything back. I didn't do anything to encourage Billy, but I think I could've discouraged him more too. I don't want to say anything that will make Max ask me any questions. I finally say in a small voice, "Okay."

"I have a work dinner tonight. Call me when you're home. And it *better* be before 9:30."

I just say a small, "Okay," again and he hangs up. I stare at my phone, sitting at a corner table for a little longer. I debate calling him back and telling him he can't talk to me like that. *But he is just doing it because he was worried about my drunk ass.*

The lingering feeling of being chastised and the guilt of disappointing him stays with me. That and the stomach flip. I can feel that I'm wet again.

I hold my forehead. *I really don't know what's come over me.* I know that I like Max, but I'm still shocked at how much I let him push me around. I smile. *He literally pushes me around in the bedroom a lot... But when I think about how controlling he is, I know I should be angry with him, but I'm not.*

His directness makes me feel safer with him than I've felt with any other guy. Like I can trust him to take care of me, to be honest with me. I don't have to second guess what he's thinking or feeling for me. He's only too happy to tell me. *And I really want to please him.*

This simple statement hangs in my head. *Please him. That's what it's come down to. Is what I'm doing pleasing Max or not.* I swallow hard. *He pushes me to please him and that's all I want to do.* I move my hand away and laugh at myself. *If Tracy could hear my thoughts, she'd kill me!*

Laura is standing in line at the counter as I get my to-go order. "Hey. I wanted to ask you...are you okay with skipping movie night tonight? Tad is coming over." She is so excited that she is actually jumping up and down a little.

I smile at her, "No. That's cool. I thought maybe you'd invite him. I do not want to be a third wheel." *And I can stop at the grocery store, do some laundry...be home early to talk to Max.* My stomach flip-flops more thinking about how pleased he'll be with me. I'm startled again by the reality of how much I care about him. *And what he thinks of me.*

23 Her

He opens the door and I immediately jump into his arms. "Happy Fourth of July. Or as I like to call it...who cares as long as it's a long weekend to celebrate."

"Our Founding Fathers would be proud of their contribution to your happiness." He's laughing as I twirl out of his arms and walk in.

I bounce back to him, putting my arms around his waist. "I look forward to the Taste and fireworks every year. And now I have a great boyfriend to share them with. I wanna celebrate."

"All right." He's still laughing, pressing our bodies tighter. "Let's go then."

"I told Tracy and Laura to meet us here, since you're so close to the Taste. And they wanted to see this place since I've been raving about it for a week."

"Okay. I'll call down to the lobby, so they will be let right up."

He takes his phone over to the sofa, and pats his lap for me to sit on while he makes the call. I snuggle into what I now think of as my spot, his arms automatically wrapping me in linen-musky warmth. When he sets the phone back down, his hand goes up the back of my shirt. "You're wearing a bikini?"

"Yeah. But I brought some clothes to change into for later too."

"But we won't be on the beach." His look is flat, eyes sharp and dark.

"No...But Tracy's boyfriend's roommates are doing this whole luau theme this year. Tiki and grass skirts. You'll see when we get to the park. She said Josh has been driving her nuts all week about it."

He doesn't say anything else, so I keep talking. "Every year, Josh's roommates put together this Taste and fireworks blow out. They arrive extra early at the park and literally stake out a large area. Last year, we had enough room for a volleyball net. Tracy said this year, they are bringing a hot tub and generator." I laugh at this, but Max just smiles slightly.

The door buzzes and I get up quickly. Max stays on the sofa.

"Hey." I yell, opening the door.

"Wow." Laura is open mouthed walking in, giving me a hug.

"Holy shit. Look at this place." Is Tracy's first words, but she's already walked past me. "Oh. Hey, Max. Great condo." He stands up as we enter the living room, a deep frown pulling his brow down.

"Thanks." Tracy is already walking towards the terrace doors, so Max follows her out.

"What a great view." Tracy and Laura are looking down and over the low wall.

"Thanks." Max stands with his legs apart and hands in his pockets. I walk over to him and put my arms around his waist again; he puts one arm around me, but remains stiff.

"Are we ready to party?" Tracy is rubbing her hands together.

"Hell ya." Laura is uncharacteristically boisterous today. She's happy to have a guy to celebrate with this year too.

I feel Max tense a little more, but he just turns and walks into the hallway. There are several bags that Tracy, Laura, and I dropped on the floor. "Let me get these." He reaches for their bags, but leaves mine. "Baby, do you need anything out of your bag for now?"

"No. I'm good. Thank you." Tracy is mouthing 'baby' behind his back. I ignore her.

It's early afternoon, but there are already over a million people here. Laura spots the flags, so we work our way through the crowd towards a large corded off area in the grass.

Even though Tracy said Billy wouldn't be here, I take a quick look around to make sure. *Good, he's not.* I don't want anything to spoil our nice day together.

Tracy sees Josh and jumps on his back. He grabs her ass from behind and bucks a little before she slides down. She pouts and points towards a large blowup pool, "I thought there was going to be a hot tub."

"Yeah. We decided that the police would probably shut a generator down from the noise and smoke. But the pool is deep."

Tracy rips off her shirt and shorts and heads towards it, dragging Josh with her. "Come on." She yells at us over her shoulder. Laura heads after them.

Max pulls my upper arm, "You're not parading around here in your bathing suit." He keeps his voice low so only I can hear him, despite the crowd. His eyes have that same steely glint.

"Um...I wasn't going to get in...I have a phobia about unclean water." I try to laugh, but it catches in my throat. He releases a little pressure, but doesn't let go of my arm.

"Good. It's not decent to run around nearly naked in public like that." He nods towards Tracy and Laura. I follow his eyes and see a group of parents and little kids next to our area. They are picking up and moving their stuff.

Suddenly I feel ashamed of our loud music, not-so-hidden drinks, bright grass-skirt covered tiki bar, and the smell of pot from a group of guys sitting on a blanket next to the pool.

"Let's get some food." Max pulls me out of the area and towards the food stalls nearby, taking my hand now.

He hasn't said anything for a while and I just keep looking up at him to see if he's no longer frowning. *So far, he's all frown.* As we turn onto another blocked-off street of stalls, I pull at his hand. "Hey. Are we going to get some food or what?" I'm smiling up at him, trying to get him to smile back. But his look remains hard.

"Lucy." He starts but then looks over my head, breathing out loudly. He starts over, "Lucy, I don't like that this is your idea of a fun time."

"I'm just hanging out with friends. That *is* fun to me." I'm hurt with his directness. His eyes narrow even more. I feel a knot in my stomach forming.

"No. You're hanging out with a bunch of stoned guys, half naked." He lifts my chin up to him. "And I don't like it."

I yank my chin away from his hand. "Can't we just have a nice day? We can walk around...and we don't have to stay here that long." I can hear the whine in my voice.

"We're *not* staying, Lucy. We're going to go back to your friends and you're going to tell them we're leaving. Now."

I look up into his face again and want to cry. His eyes and mouth are set so hard. My stomach is doing back-flips now in response, but my head is trying to make sense of everything. *I want to please him...but I've looked forward to this day for a while.*

I suddenly feel a hand on my shoulder and jump with a small squeak. A homeless guy is touching my back. Max reacts quickly and pushes himself between the guy and me. "Something I can help you with?" The guy waves his hands in front of Max like an umpire calling safe. "Then move along...Sir." Max waits until he's walked away before turning around to me again.

"Are you okay?" His look is soft and concerned now. I put my arms around him and press my face against his shirt. He rubs my head and kisses the top. "Come on. Let's go." I feel safe in his powerful arms and know that he's just looking out for me.

Returning to the corded area, I feel pretty good about leaving early. Josh's roommates are loudly judging a hula contest between two drunk girls in one corner, the stoners haven't moved, and Tracy and Josh are making out in the pool. I don't see Laura anywhere. Max doesn't cross the cord, just stands with his hands in his pockets again. I squeeze his arm, saying, "I'll be right back."

I head over to Tracy. "Hey. We're going to take off."

"What?" Tracy splashes water towards me.

"Yeah. Max isn't into the pot smoking crowd," I point a thumb over my shoulder towards the blanket. "Where's Laura?"

"She went for food with Tad. I'll tell her you bailed on us for Gramps over there." She splashes again, just missing me.

"Not funny." I reach in and splash her back, jumping away before she can try again. "I'll call you tomorrow. Have fun."

Walking back to Max, the knot in my stomach tightens. He smiles and drapes his arm around my shoulders, putting me at ease. "How bout we eat our way back to my place?"

"Sounds good to me." And I put my arm around his waist again.

24 Him

It feels good sitting around my coffee table; Lucy is in my t-shirt again, pizza cheese stretching between her and a plate. I smile remembering her mouth around my cock earlier. We spent hours exploring each other. She responded to my every touch and need. She was especially eager to please me.

Lucy keeps surprising me. I thought she might give me shit about making her leave her friends. She looked so torn when I told her we were leaving. I thought she might speak up then.

But she seemed to be happy to get away from the crowds, as much as I was. She was only a little defensive when I said her friends shouldn't act so wild. That their boyfriends shouldn't let them. But even then, she remained quiet and didn't argue with me.

It's been so easy between us, that I'm almost afraid of what I feel for her. I want to have faith in our connection so far. How she's responded every step of the way; she's been pliant and giving. No arguments, no talking back, just giving in to me, giving herself to me.

I fear that it's only because she doesn't really care about me, about us. *Maybe, she's not pushing back because she's just having fun and it doesn't matter what I say or do?*

But I don't really believe this. I know this is just old fears of what went wrong in the past. I've been more controlling with Lucy from the start. Guiding her with small rules to follow, slowly opening up about myself and what I want, pushing us into a deeper connection each time. She has been responsive, even anticipating my demands, all along. She even said herself that she liked that I was in control. *But that was when she was drunk.*

Outside, there's a boom. "Hey. The fireworks." Lucy jumps up, her tits jiggling nicely under the shirt. "Can we see anything from here?" She's heading towards the terrace and I follow behind her, the night air feeling cold on my exposed chest.

We can just see the tops of firework explosions, the clouds all around turning a kaleidoscope of colors.

"Not a good night for it." She sounds disappointed, but she squeezes my arms around her. "I love this terrace."

"I love you." I whisper this into her hair. She turns around to face me.

"You do?" Her look sends shockwaves to my cock again, her eyes wide and pleading.

"Yes." I kiss her open lips, pushing my tongue around hers.

"I love you too, Max." Her eyes are wet.

And I know that I haven't been wrong. She is the girl for me.

25 Her

Isn't there a song about all the love songs having more meaning when you're in love? That's how I feel. Cloud frickin' 9. Yesterday, I fell asleep snuggled in his arms, head on his chest, waking in the middle of the night and still in the same spot.

I'm wide awake now, but Max isn't in bed with me anymore. I pull on his t-shirt, smiling that he'd insisted we sleep naked together, his warmth more than enough for me.

I find him in the kitchen, on the phone. He waves me over to him and pulls me into a side hug, kissing my head. He mouths "coffee" and nods towards a counter.

"...So when will you be back?" He is listening intently on the phone, his eyes on me though. "Okay. Next Saturday then. We'll come up there." More listening. "All right. I'll take care of that, Sir. Have a safe trip. And give my love to Mom."

"Was that your stepdad?" I put more sweetener into the trucker-strength coffee.

"Yeah...My *dad*." He stresses the word, so I know he prefers not to call him 'step.' "His business trip is set a little early, but we're going to go up there next weekend, so you can meet my family."

I practically spit out my sip of coffee, burning my lip a little. "You want me to meet your family?"

"Of course. I met yours." He says this so matter-of-factly, leaning against his counter with his arms crossed. His arm and chest muscles stand out more.

"Yeah...but that was because they were in town. Not a specific trip to meet them. Where do your folks live?"

He puts his arms out for me to come to him, wrapping them around me. "It's not far. They live in Evanston; but over the summer, they have a lake house in Wisconsin."

"And you want to go there next weekend? With me?"

"Yes...I want them to meet you." He fills my mouth with kisses before I can say anything more. "We'll head out early Saturday and come home late Sunday."

"We'll stay the night there?" I'm nervous about spending the whole weekend around his family. "What will the sleeping arrangements be?"

He half smiles at this. "Are you worried about what they'll think of you if we sleep in the same room?" He's teasing me, kissing my nose. "You are so cute."

"Yes. I can tell you that we would *not* be sleeping together at *my* dad's house!" I push his chest a little. "I think it's too soon for this...for me."

His jaw clenches for just a second. "Why don't you let me worry about that?" I let myself melt into his kisses again.

"I'm an adult. My parents wouldn't expect you to sleep anywhere else except with me."

"I thought your family was so old fashioned…" I say this into his chest, still nervously thinking about next weekend.

"They are. That's why my girl would be by my side." He kisses my head again, breathing warmth onto my hair. "I wouldn't take any risks with you. It's important to me that they like you. So trust me, okay?"

"Okay...but you'll have to keep talking me into this all week." I push against him again. He laughs and I feel his body shake against mine.

"How bout I entice you into it? I'll take you shopping today for some new dresses you can show off." He squeezes my ass and doesn't let go, lifting me towards him.

"What's wrong with this? It's a dress on me." I'm laughing since his t-shirt comes almost to my knees.

"And you're beautiful in it." He picks me up so my legs go around his waist, my hands twining his hair, his hands cupping my ass. "I need food, girl, before round two!" His smile is big and all for me.

"I think you mean round four...*teen*!" I lightly bite his neck before he puts me down.

26 Her

"Hey. Come out so we can see you." I'm trying to zip up in the dressing room, but can hear Max around the corner. I get the dress most of the way up and come out. Max is standing with a saleswoman in front of the loungers and tall mirrors.

I've never shopped in Needless Markup before. *I'm having a very princess-y in a movie moment.* Standing in front of the mirrors, Max finishes zipping me up and I ask him, "What do you think?" The dress is more ladylike than I would usually choose, a blue and white seersucker material with large crisscrossing straps in the back, just above my knees.

The saleswoman answers first, "We need to take in the waist a little, but this is easy with the darts and seams boning here." She stands next to me and pulls the dress in the back to lie flat against me.

"Perfect." Max is all smiles. "Cassandra, can you pick out a few more options for her try on?"

"Of course. What is the occasion?" They are talking around me, while I continue looking at the dress from different angles.

"A weekend getaway. We're heading to the lake next Saturday."

"So, dresses, skirts, shorts, and tops?" She is already turning away.

"No shorts." Max calls after her. She turns around again and just nods. I know Max prefers me in something very feminine. I'm used to his demands about what I wear already. Laura said she thought it was so sweet that he cares that much to comment on my clothes; Tracy said he must be gay for caring about clothes that much at all. I didn't really tell them just how demanding he has been though. Making me change out of several of my favorite outfits, deemed too revealing or not girly enough for his tastes.

"Do you like it?" He is standing behind me again.

Turning around to face him from my dais, I am closer to his height and put my arms around his shoulders. "Yes. I feel very grown-up, garden party, mint julep sipping in this." I kiss him. "But you really don't need to buy me a dress. I have lots of summer stuff to wear."

"I am going to buy you a whole new wardrobe for next weekend. I want you to feel special. To know how special you are to me."

"Hmm... Or it is that you want your parents to be impressed with me?" I squint up at him with a pressed lip smile.

"That too." He kisses my frown away. "It's a weekend retreat, but they are more formal people. I want you to feel comfortable, to not worry about fitting in."

I turn to look at myself in the mirror again.

Hmm...Maybe he has a point. If this is a dress that fits in with his parent's crowd, then I definitely don't have anything quite like it in my closet. All my clothes are either super casual or business.

Cassandra returns with a salesgirl, both their arms are loaded down with clothes. "Wow. That's a lot to try on."

She laughs and says, "These are only the dresses. I'll return with a few shirt and skirt options too."

"You better get started." Max is shaking his head at me, chuckling.

Sipping champagne under the rotunda, my princess moment just keeps going. Max picked out four dresses, four shirts, and three skirts, way more than I would possibly need for an overnight trip. A seamstress came into the dressing room to tailor everything just for me. They said it would all be ready by the time we finished our lunch upstairs.

"I can't believe how patient you were during that marathon fashion show, especially for a guy who hates to wait for cabs even." I tip my flute towards him.

He gives a wicked grin. "Well...I was patiently waiting for the next part." He raises one eyebrow and sips the last of his wine.

"Why am I suddenly afraid?" I'm laughing.

"You'll need new lingerie to go with all those new clothes..." His smile is huge.

"Oh God. I am *not* trying on a bunch of lacy stuff for you and some saleswoman!" The thought of walking out of a dressing room in nothing but a bra and thong makes me cringe in my chair.

"No. But you will have to pick out some things to show me later...in private." His brow is arched again.

27 Her

"...So how much did he end up spending on you?" I'd been telling Laura about my weekend with Max while we waited for Tracy to show up for drinks.

"I'm not even sure. He paid for everything while I was busy with the seamstress. It was crazy. I felt like I was in a movie."

"What movie?" Tracy finally arrives and plops her bag down on the table.

"Max took her shopping and bought all these clothes for her." Laura blurts out.

"How very Pretty...wasn't she a whore in that movie?" Laura rolls her eyes at Tracy.

I take a sip of my drink before snarking back, "Isn't that high praise coming from you?"

Laura fills us in on her weekend with Tad. She spent Friday night with him, then went to his softball game on

Saturday. "Billy was on his team. He asked about you." She looks at me over the rim of her beer.

"I hope you told him I have a boyfriend now. He didn't seem to believe me last time."

"No...I just asked what happened between you guys. He said he acted stupid and asked me to apologize to you for him." She downs a gulp of beer. "What did happen?"

"He wouldn't get off of me in the cab home. I told him I was seeing someone and he just laughed and called me a tease."

"What a fucking asshole punk." Tracy is ever the artist.

"Huh. Well he seemed sincere. I thought he was sweet..." Laura doesn't like conflict.

"Not sweet. Asshole." Tracy downs her drink.

"Well, it doesn't matter now. And Tad's not an asshole, so who cares?" I don't want Laura to feel badly about one of Tad's friends. She's wanted a guy in her life for so long, I wouldn't want to ruin it for her.

"Tad *is* a sweetheart." She's all bubbly again. "Hey. I just realized. We'll all have dates for Romona's for the first time."

Tracy cheers her empty glass against ours. "Assuming Gramps will be okay with that…"

I shove her shoulder. "You better not call him that Wednesday."

"I'll be on my best behavior. I promise." She crosses her heart. "So...will he be bringing a joint or should Josh bring his bong?" She erupts in laughter as I attack tickle her side, Laura pushes her into me.

Tonight is going great. Josh and Tracy aren't falling all over each other for once. Tad is being so sweet to Laura that her face looks like it's going to break from smiling. And Max is the perfect gentleman, holding open doors and pulling out my chair for me. Rosa comes over with our breadsticks and we introduce her to Tad and Max.

Max stands and shakes her hand. She makes an impressed face towards me and gives an 'okay' sign with a nod. Tracy rolls her eyes, but Tad stands up too after that. Laura beams.

"So you girls want the usual." Rosa is clapping her hands together. "How bout you boys?"

Max answers, "Lucy and I will share your Puttanesca with a side of garlic spinach."

Rosa and Tracy raise their eyebrows at the same time. Rosa turns to me, "You sure, honey? You girls always get the spaghetti and meatballs to split."

"Um...Yeah. I can have some of the meatballs too." Max is watching me closely. He puts his hand on my knee under the table and gives a small squeeze while leaning over to kiss my cheek.

Max returns from the bathroom and stands behind my chair. "Baby, you ready to go?"

"We're just waiting on the check still." Josh and Tracy are counting the money we've pooled in front of them. "I threw in our portion." For some reason, it feels weird saying this to him. I realize that this is the first time I've paid for one of our dates. Even though I've offered to chip in before, he always refuses to let me pay for anything.

"I took care of the bill already." He pulls my chair a little, so I stand up.

Josh looks up at this. "You didn't have to do that, Max." He kisses Tracy. "Now what are we going to argue about on the way home?" He shakes his head at Max, "Man, you ruined makeup sex night." Tracy hits his chest, but she's laughing with him.

"Thanks." Laura is already putting her money back in her wallet and giving Tad and me our share back from the pool too.

"Yeah. Thank you, sweetie." I kiss his cheek.

We all walk out together. Max stops to shake hands again with Rosa and her husband, raving about their sauces. Rosa is proudly waving at us, "See you girls next week. Be good…"

Outside, Jeff is waiting for us with the car door open. "Does anyone want a ride? We're heading south." Max offers.

Josh and Tracy are already walking down the street. Josh answers walking backwards, "No, thanks. We're heading to Mullihan's. Anyone wanna join us?"

Tracy adds, "I'm going to kick his fucking ass at pool so we have something to fight about." Josh grabs her around the waist and tries to pick her up, but she pushes him off, both laughing loudly. Laura and Tad follow behind them, holding hands.

I look up at Max and see his jaw clenched. I know his answer without asking. I wave them off, "Have fun. I'll see you tomorrow."

Max doesn't relax his jaw in the car. I put my head on his shoulder, waiting for him to say whatever he's thinking. Finally, he breathes deeply and relaxes a little. "That girl has quite a mouth on her." I knew it had something to do with Tracy. She had been nice, but a little edgy with him all night.

"Yeah. Cursing's an art form with her." I shrug my shoulder against him.

"Josh shouldn't allow her talk like that." I know without looking that his eyes match his steely voice.

"Ha. I'd like to see him try to stop her." I laugh at the image in my head. "She's not likely to change for anyone."

He squeezes my hand harder. "Just so you don't talk like that."

I look up at him and try for a seductive fluttering of lashes, whispering, "What? Don't you want a girl who can talk dirty to you?"

His look only hardens. "No, Lucy. I'm serious. I won't tolerate that from you." He doesn't look away and I feel that heat in the pit of my stomach, spreading down again.

"Well...I've heard you curse before..." I swallow loudly, but keep his gaze.

"I'm a man."

I can't believe he just said that! "So...?"

"So. A girl has to be careful with how she's perceived in this world. If you talk like a fucking whore, then you'll be treated like one." He lightly brushes my cheek with his finger. "And I would never let that happen." He kisses my forehead.

"That's a very misogynistic view of the world, don't you think?" But I say this quietly, looking down at our joined hands. I feel confused. *Part of me wants to call him an asshole and jump out of the car and another part of me thinks he's chivalrous.* I've had these warring thoughts before when he says things like this.

"Yes. It is." When I look up at him though, his smile is tender. I decide to let it go and just lean against his shoulder again.

28 Him

With my hand on Lucy's knee, I let out the deep breath I'd been holding before turning the car off. She looks great, her figure on display. She's still modest though in the form-fitting yellow dress, eyes bright, smile big, and her face in full view with her hair pulled back.

"You ready?" I squeeze her knee. We'd been talking about how nervous she is for the last half hour of the drive up. She swallows and nods. "Stay there." I stop her from opening her door. She's still getting used to that rule.

Walking around to her side, I put my hand out to help her stand. Behind me, I can hear the front door opening. "You'll be fine." I quickly kiss Lucy before turning towards the porch.

"Max." Mom is hurrying down the stairs with her arms wide-open. She kisses my cheek and quickly rubs off any lipstick. Ron joins her side, his arm going around her. We shake hands first, then he pulls me forward for a quick one-armed hug, too.

"Mom, Dad. This is Lucy." I stand back so they can see her.

Mom puts her hands on Lucy's shoulders and gives her a small hug this way. "Welcome, Lucy."

"Yes. Welcome to our home, Lucy." Dad gives her forearm a squeeze at the same time. "I'm Ron; this is Alex."

"Thank you for having me." Lucy's voice is even higher than normal. I put my arm around her shoulders.

"I hope you kids are hungry. I've been cooking and baking all morning." Mom leads the way inside.

Their lake house is shaker-style, a blown-out bungalow with wide doorways, dark polished floors, shutters on all the windows. The back of the house has a great view from every room, french doors open to let the lake breeze in, beachy colors of sand and blues throughout. "It smells great in here, Mom."

"I'm starving." Lucy couldn't eat breakfast; she was too nervous about this trip. We follow my dad into the family room off the kitchen.

"Why don't you help my mom, baby?" I nod towards the adjoining kitchen. She hesitates for a second before walking through the dining area. By the look of Lucy's unused appliances, I'm not even sure she knows what to do in a kitchen. *This could be interesting.* I can hear my mom directing her to bring a platter over to the stove. *So far so good.*

Dad claps his hand on my shoulder. "So did you have any trouble filing the Standosh papers this week?"

"No. But we didn't get them back yet, either. I think you're looking at a big mess, Dad."

Lucy walks in with two beers. "Um...your mom thought you guys would like these." She hands one to each of us.

"Thanks, baby." I kiss her head.

"Thank you, Lucy," Dad tips his bottle to her and continues our conversation as she walks back towards the kitchen.

"Yeah. Robbie has himself in another mess that's for sure. We'll be able to bill some nice hours out of this one." He takes a swig and I follow him out to the back patio. The sound of the waves against the dock is distant but soothing. "She seems like a nice girl." He gestures back to the house with his bottle. "How long have you two been dating?"

"Long enough. Sir." I take a big drink. "And she is really nice."

He doesn't say anything for a while, just stares out at the water. "Since you haven't brought a girl around to meet us in a while..." He turns to face me. "I assume you're serious about her."

"I am."

"And..." His face is thoughtful, the lawyer trying to find the best phrasing. "And she isn't like that other girl, Natalie?"

"No." I shake my head and look him direct in the eye. I'm still embarrassed about how it ended with her. "No, Lucy's different. I think you'll really like her when you get to know her more." I take a drink before adding, "I can be myself with her."

"Good." He claps my shoulder again. "It's important for a man to have a happy home that he can be himself in."

"Lunch is ready, boys." Mom is standing in the doorway with Lucy just behind her.

"Let's eat out here, Alex." Dad takes a seat at the outdoor cedar table.

"But I have the dining table all set in here for us." Mom is ringing her hands. I don't need to turn around to know that Dad has given her The Look. Her face freezes and she quickly adds, "But it is so nice out here. It'll only take me a minute to set up." She turns so quickly around that she nearly knocks over Lucy. "Oh, sorry, dear. Would you like to help me move things outside?" She's already moving quickly around the table, picking up dishes.

Lucy looks questioningly at me, but turns slowly to help my mom with the table. I sit down and watch her. I can see Dad's face out of the corner of my eye. He hasn't relaxed yet.

The Look is what my brother, Jake, and I called it as kids. When his eyes would deepen, his jaw would harden, his brows would grow in depth. You just knew you were in trouble if you got The Look.

"Lucy, can you get me another beer, baby?" I hand her my empty as she puts plates and silverware on the table. "Dad...you need another?" He hands his empty to her too. She isn't saying anything, but I can see her mind working, questioning all this.

Mom is finally setting the last dish down next to Dad. He relaxes and puts his arm around her hips, "This looks great, honey." Mom visibly relaxes too. "Dig in."

Dad pours wine for Lucy and passes the bottle to me to pour some in Mom's glass. "Cheers to our son and his very nice girlfriend, Lucy."

Lucy finally smiles again. "Thank you. And cheers to you both for having us up this weekend." She takes a big gulp.

Walking with Lucy along the retaining wall of my parent's property, her hand feels warm in mine. "So what do you think of my mom and dad?" She didn't say much after lunch, but volunteered to help clear the table. Mom insisted we go for a walk while she cleaned up though.

"They're nice." She squeezes into my side more, our legs walking in harmony on the grass.

"But...?" I can tell she's holding back. I want to push this conversation with her.

"But. Are they always so intense?" She laughs to try to take the edge off of what she said.

"My dad is an intense guy. He's had to be. He was orphaned at the age of ten and had to make due for himself. He's proud of what he's accomplished in life so far and he really instilled in all of us that same sense of pride. I try to live up to what he expects of me." I'm getting closer to the heart of why I brought her here.

"But your mom is tense too. I thought she was walking on eggshells today."

"No. Well...Maybe a little. But she knows how my dad expects things to be and tries her hardest to please him." I glance quickly at her to see her reaction. Her face remains relaxed and deep in thought. *Good.* "It's how I would want my wife to be."

Now she does look up at me. I can tell she doesn't know what to say to this, so I continue. "I told you before that my dad was strict with us. That includes my mom."

She stops walking and sits on the wall. I sit next to her, facing the lake, the warmth of the sun on our backs. She still says nothing, so I cautiously keep talking. "Lucy, I brought you up here not just to meet my parents, but to see how I was raised."

She finds her voice finally. "My dad was strict too, Max... But what do you mean by with your mom?"

"I mean he had rules that we all followed." I wait for her response. It's important to gauge how she's reacting. I'm glad that we're alone, far away from anyone. I need to hear what she really thinks. I never took the time to talk this way with any other girlfriend.

"Like what?"

"Well...like not talking back." I keep my voice even, my arm around her waist.

She doesn't say anything for a while, just twists her fingers together. "My dad was sort of strict too. With me more than PJ..." She trails off, looking down at her fingers. I cover her hands with mine. "He had certain rules too, but I don't think they applied to my mom."

"I see something in you, Lucy. Something that I respond to..." my voice is deep with emotion, gravelly. "I told you that I want to be myself with you. A big part of that is you understanding where I come from." I put my hand on the side of her head and turn her face towards me. "I love you. And I want us to be honest with each other."

"I want that too." Her eyes are bright with wetness. I kiss her and end with my mouth on her hair, breathing in her scent.

I decide to not push anymore. Her response has been better than I could've expected so far. "Let's head back." I get up and put my hand out to lift her up. Before heading up the stairs to the patio, I pull her in for a full kiss.

Sitting around the table, dinner cleared. Dad pulls out his 31 year old Glendronach and pours me a tumbler. Mom puts down a backgammon set in front of me. "Do you remember how to play?" She's smiling down on me, hand on my back.

"Of course."

"Does he remember how to lose, you mean?" Dad is sitting opposite me again, pulling up his sleeves and setting up the game.

"Why don't you teach Lucy how to play, Dad? I'm going to get our luggage." I stand up and Lucy gives me a pleading look. I kiss her head.

"Great. New blood," Dad responds, rubbing his hands together. "Lucy?" He turns the board to be in front of her instead.

Mom sits next to her, "I'll help you. So he doesn't cheat." Mom squeezes her forearm.

"I played with my aunt before. But I don't think I remember all the nuances." Lucy takes a big sip of her red wine.

Coming back inside, I carry our luggage upstairs. The laughter from Mom and Lucy follows me. I can hear Dad protesting something. I remember a lot of family room hours spent around learning games with him.

29 Her

I take a last look at myself in the mirror. *Not bad.* Max said he didn't want to see any of the lingerie on me until tonight. This push-up baby-doll top and matching thong doesn't cover much, the white lace strategically placed over my nipples and the top hardly covering my ass cheeks. I had to shave my bikini line extra thin to not be poking out of the sides of the barely-there thong. I smile thinking how much Max will like this. I fluff my hair and wet my lips. *Ready as I'll ever be.*

"Hey. You going to stay in there all night?" Max yells from the bedroom. I quickly turn off the light and come out of the bathroom.

"Shhh. They might hear you." I loudly whisper.

"They can't hear us. They're on the other end of the hall." He sits up in bed, swinging his legs over the side. "Stop. I want to get a good look at you."

I freeze two steps away from him while he looks me up and down. I stare at him too. He's naked and his cock is standing upright, the size of him still startling to me. "Turn around. Okay. Now you can come here."

I bound over to the bed, standing between his legs, my arms around his neck.

"Put your arms behind your back." His face is buried in my neck and hair, nibbling and tickling with his stubble. I feel my stomach twinge.

I cross my arms in back, and he pulls me towards him more, moving both hands to the sides of my face. He gives me a wicked grin. "On your knees." I awkwardly try to lower myself, but move my arms to use the bed for support. "No. Keep your arms back." His sharpness makes me stop for a second, but his grin is still there and he puts his hands on my arms to help me down.

Kneeling in front of him now, his cock is even thicker and bigger, inches from my face. I look up at him and wait for him to say what I know is next. "Open your mouth." I comply. He puts his cock in between my open lips with his hand, then moves his hands to the sides of my face again.

I can taste his saltiness and move my tongue around his tip and length. He moans and pushes into me more. I back away, choking a little. "No." He keeps me still with one hand on the back of my head, but isn't pushing into me again. I can only look up at him. His warning eyes make me even wetter.

He slowly pushes into me, keeping his eyes locked with mine. I try not to gag and breathe through my nose. "Tighten your lips around me." I comply again and he pulls out, scraping against my back teeth slightly, my tongue lapping around him. He moans softly. He keeps slowly entering my mouth and pulling back; each time deep and causing me to gag a little, but not letting me move away.

I'm aware of only the wetness on my thong, his cock, my tongue, his eyes. Everything else has faded to black. He pulls out completely and I keep my mouth open for a second longer, my jaw a little sore. His hand in the back of my hair pulls my head back sharply and I gasp. "Stand up." He pulls me up, using his hand to pull on my hair. I stand quickly, keeping my arms back. He smiles at me, but his hand gives one final yank of my head before letting go.

He grabs my arm, pulling it from behind my back and pushes me onto the bed, face down. My legs hang over the sides. I turn my head to see him, moving my hand to push my hair away from my face. "No. Behind your back again." I quickly move my arms to comply. He yanks the thong down my legs.

Grabbing my hips, he drags me further off the bed, my legs dangling more, my pussy exposed. I blush knowing he can see how wet he's made me already. He grips my thighs and pulls them apart, entering me with such suddenness and force that I cry out. From this position, I am helpless to stop him from pushing in too deep, his cock ramming my pussy. His fingers dig into my hips and ass, pulling himself into me more with each thrust.

I bury my face in the bed, my screams a mix of pain and pleasure, loud to my own ears. Max doesn't stop ramming into me until I think I can't take anymore. His legs shake and he falls onto me as we come together.

Max stays deep inside me, his whole body pressing painfully on my arms until the last of his cock spasms. He stands up, but doesn't pull out. He keeps one hand on my crossed arms, pinning me to the bed still.

"Did you come?"

"...Yes..." It's a hoarse whisper.

"Good girl." He still doesn't leave me though. I can feel him hardening again. "Squeeze me."

"...I can't..." my throat sore from screaming into the covers, "I'm too sore."

"I said squeeze me." He pulls my arms up, sending a painful jolt to my shoulders. I gasp and squeeze him at the same time. "That's my good girl." He slowly starts rocking into me, his cock hardening fast. "Stay tight around me." I'm gasping with the effort.

He starts full speed fucking me. I stop trying to grasp him inside me, my own spasms of come squeezing him deeper. He comes again, standing up, pressed deep to me. He waits till I've stopped spasming before pulling out. I remain on the bed with my arms behind me for a second longer. I don't trust moving, my head is spinning.

"So what do your folks think of me?" I'm lying in his arms, staring out the french doors, all the stars glittering over the water. My voice is still hoarse, my pussy still throbbing.

"I can tell my mom really likes you. She smiles a lot at you and gave you a big hug before heading to bed." He sounds sleepy, yawning. "My dad said he's happy that I found such a nice girl."

"He told you that? When?" Despite the long drive and my nerves all day, I'm not tired. I don't want him to fall asleep just yet.

He adjusts his shoulder under my head and wakes himself up a bit more. "Yeah. When you were helping Mom with dessert. He said you were nice and polite. And that you obviously cared about me a lot." He nudges my head with his shoulder.

"I do." I'm happy that this weekend is going so well. I still feel weird about sleeping together with them just down the hall, but they really didn't seem to mind. His mom even said she put extra towels and two robes in the bathroom if we needed them.

"Good. Because I care a lot about you, Lucy." He kisses my head and I kiss his chest again. "And I want you to be comfortable around my family."

"They didn't seem as tense tonight." His hand stroking my head is starting to make me sleepy too. The stress of the day melting from me.

"I'm sure my dad talked to my mom while we were out for our walk." I close my eyes listening to the low rumble of his voice against my ear on his chest. This is just as I imagined, his voice in the dark.

"Talked to her about what…?" I try to keep my eyes open.

"Her behavior." The twinge in my stomach awakens me more, alerted by how his heartbeat quickens slightly, even as his hand continues its rhythmic movement through my hair and his voice remains steady.

"What do you mean?"

"How bout we talk about this in the morning..." He kisses my head again. I shift so my face is up to his even though I can barely see him in the dark.

"No...Say what you want to say. Please?" I kiss his chest. He moves his arm from under me and rolls over.

I blink against the small bedside lamp he turned on. "If we're going to have this conversation, I want to be able to see you."

"What conversation?" We're both sitting up now. He props pillows up against the rustic wood headboard and puts out his arm for me to sit back against him again. I curl into his chest, so I can see his face.

"I told you that I was adopted by Ron, me and my brother were." I nod my head, putting my arm around his stomach. "Well...my mom wasn't married to our deadbeat dad. She was very young when she had us...and kinda...wild I guess is the best way of saying it. Deadbeat left when I was four, Jake was only one." His breathing is steady, but his heartbeat sounds louder.

"That must have been hard for you and your mom." Most of my friends are children of divorce, so I know a lot about broken homes, even though my parents stayed married.

"Yeah. I don't really remember Deadbeat. I saw him once when I was six. He came through town and tried to stay with us. He had baseball gloves for us that were too big. I threw them both away. Mom met Ron the next year and he became our real dad." I don't interrupt him as his words keep tumbling out.

"The first seven years of my life were pretty bad." I stroke his chest and stomach. Seeing the pain in his eyes, I touch his cheek too. He takes my hand and kisses my palm, smiling at me. "I'm okay now. I just want you to know everything."

"Okay... Go on."

"My mom had a hard life. Her parents kicked her out when she got pregnant with me; she didn't finish high school even. Deadbeat couldn't hold a job and I think they both were doing drugs. After he left, she waitressed at several places. She was always tired...always angry. She took that out on Jake and me."

I can't believe the same sweet woman from today is who he's talking about now. "Your mom hurt you?"

"I was able to protect Jake for the most part. But that meant that I got the brunt of it...her anger at whatever." He shrugs and I move with him. "It's all in the past now."

"So... She's not like that now?" I trace circles into his light chest hair.

"No." He pushes out a small laugh. "Not since Ron." He pauses for so long, I think I may need to prompt him to say more. But then he continues, his voice even deeper, stronger.

"Ron showed my mom how to be a good woman. A good wife and mother. He didn't allow her to discipline us." I was no longer looking up at him, but I could feel his head turned down to me, his words moving little hairs on my head.

"So your mom didn't hurt you guys anymore after she married Ron?" I can picture Max as a little boy and I just want to hug him.

"No. She tried once in front of him, before they married. She was embarrassed I think because Jake wasn't listening to her about something. She went to smack Jake and Ron grabbed her wrist. He sent us to our room, but I listened with the door cracked. I couldn't hear everything; Jake was crying in his bed, scared. But I heard enough. Mom was never the same after that. And neither were we."

I wait for Max to tell me the rest, but he stays quiet for so long, I look up into his face again. His eyes are far away and veiled for a second, but then they clear and look directly into mine.

"So what did he say to your mom that changed everything?"

"He told her that she wasn't being a good woman. That she needed a man...him...in her life. That it was his job to discipline as the man of the house." He pauses, brushing my hair away from my cheek, holding my chin up towards him. "Then he led her into her room. I crept out of ours and stood outside her door so I could hear the rest."

"What did you hear?" I swallow, my chin held up making it louder, but I don't move away from his hand.

"I heard him spanking my mom. I think they were married a few weeks after that." *I can't believe I heard him right!* He continues staring at me, looking back and forth between my eyes.

"I...I don't know what to say." I finally move my head away from his hand and look down. "I..."

"I told you I wanted you to know everything. So you'll understand where I come from. And how I think." He gently pulls my face back up to him, but doesn't hold my chin.

"How you think? You think it's okay that your stepdad spanked your mom?"

"Yes." I can only blink in response to this. "I think that she was finally able to be the person she was always meant to be...a loving, caring mom and wife."

"Because he spanked her?" I sit back from him, to face him fully.

He takes my hand and I don't pull it away, just stare at our joined fingers. "He did more than that. He showed us how to be a family, how to love and respect each other. Jake and I finally had a stable home, with a mom who never hurt us and a dad who really cared about us."

"Did he spank you?" *I still can't believe I'm hearing this*. I'm staring at him again, but our fingers remain locked.

He continues to speak in the same low and steady voice. "Yes. When we needed it, he would discipline us." I start to pull away, but he pulls on my hand. "Hey. He wasn't a monster." He smiles at me and shakes my hand to get me to look up at him again. "He wasn't crazy angry like my mom was. He set rules for all of us to follow and if we didn't, then we knew the consequences." He shakes my hand once more, my fingers feeling sweaty against his. "Are you telling me that your dad never spanked you?"

"Well...yeah...when I was really little maybe. But never my mom." Now I'm staring into his eyes, back and forth.

"Lucy, I want you to understand. This is who I am. This is how I expect it to be with *us*." He says it so deeply, it's almost a whisper.

I jump out of bed and go to the bathroom, shutting the door quickly and standing against its coolness. I don't even turn on the light.

30 Him

I can see the light's finally on, a sliver under the bathroom door. I haven't heard much movement, but know that I need to give her this time to think.

I had planned to tell her all this on the way home tomorrow. Laughing to myself, *now that probably was a bad idea. What if she had jumped out of the moving car?*

I wait with the light on for her to come out, still sitting propped up in bed. I try not to think about how much it'll hurt if she comes out and packs her bag.

I keep telling myself that this was a necessary step. I realized after the bad breakup with Natalie that it wasn't going to be easy to find the right girl for me. Natalie's reaction the first time I tried to discipline her was to call the cops. We'd been out to a party and her drinking and flirting had been too much for me to take. She was obviously drunk, so the cops just let me off with a warning after Natalie calmed down and left.

I tried to reach out to Nat the next day, thinking after she sobered up we might be able to talk it through. She threatened to call the cops again if I ever tried to see her. *I never want to go through that again.*

I felt something different with Lucy from the moment I met her. *She's so soft-spoken, sweet...she responds so easily to my commands in bed...and for the most part, out of bed too.* I try to calm my breathing. *One way or another, I have to see this through tonight and hope for the best.*

A half hour goes by before she finally opens the door, turning off the light. She stands at the doorway, not moving, crossing her legs and holding the door jam.

I pat the bed next to me. "Come here." *Now's the moment of truth.*

She pushes herself away from the door and slowly walks over to me. The robe she has on is dragging the floor, only her fingers visible in the rolled-up sleeves, holding the ties at her waist. She sits on the edge of the bed with her back to me for a minute before twisting around to face me more.

Her eyes search mine. "I don't know what to say to you."

"I love you. How bout that?" I give her a bright grin. She only lowers her face, so her hair veils around her. I reach out, covering her hand with mine. "I *do* love you, Lucy."

"And I love you, Max." She chokes this out, a whispered confession in one long breath.

"That's all that matters." I pull her hand, trying to get her to look up or move closer to me.

"No. It isn't. I don't know if I can be what you want..."

"*I* know you can." She does look up at this, responding to the demand in my voice. *Good girl.* "I told you before that I see something in you. From the beginning I've known that we can be great together. I know your heart is sweet and good. And all mine." This time I pull her forearm and she follows, moving across the bed to sit next to me. Her arms wrap around her knees, still guarded though. I wrap my arms around hers, rocking her gently, kissing her head lightly. "Baby, just say you're willing to give me a chance. That's all I need tonight."

"Okay..." Her voice is tiny, muffled into her knees.

I continue rocking, stroking her hair until her breathing matches mine. "That's my girl." We fall asleep with her curled up in the big robe, in my arms.

31 Her

The sun shines in from the french doors. I turn just my head to see if Max is in bed with me. He's not. I sit up and look to the bathroom door. He's not there either. I get out of bed, the robe twisted around me making it difficult. Looking out the french doors onto the terrace, I still don't see Max.

I head to the bathroom and change into the only shorts and tank top I have. Putting my hair in a loose knot and brushing my teeth, I try to think about our conversation again.

I still can't figure out how I feel. I'm stunned at what he revealed, but not truly surprised. He'd been saying all week how much this trip meant to him. *Now I know why*. He waited till now to say all that, about his family, himself.

I stare in the mirror, the same way I did last night. If I'm honest with myself, I knew that Max was different before he said anything. I let out a shaky laugh. *I just had no idea how different!*

Other guys I've dated have all been easy-going, not decisive, not demanding, and really not for me. I remember saying to Tracy how frustrating guys can be, never wanting to make a plan, never choosing the restaurant or movie, never taking charge. She laughed at me and said she preferred it that way. The metro-guy was her type. Not mine.

My last semi-serious boyfriend ended with me leaving him at a club because he wouldn't commit to staying over. I smile at myself thinking of how Max would react if I tried to leave him somewhere. *He'd probably spank me.* I let out another small laugh. *Oh, God, this is still all too surreal for me...*

I came out of the bathroom last night after realizing that no matter what Max thought of how he was raised, he was a reasonable man, a loving man. And I wasn't anything like his mom had been, *wild he had said.* I was good, *sweet he had said.*

Again, if I'm honest with myself, I've liked his controlling nature too. *For the most part.* I always know where I stand with him. He's direct and tells me exactly what he wants. I smile. *I mean what he demands.*

Taking a deep breath, I leave the bedroom. I can't hear anything downstairs. *Maybe they're all gone?* But I do smell the wonderful scent of something baking and much needed coffee.

Walking into the family room, I stop at the door to the patio. Alex is sitting on Ron's lap, facing away from me, but I can tell they're kissing. I don't think I've ever seen my own parents kiss, so I feel really awkward and start to turn around.

"Oh. Good morning, Lucy." Alex is standing up when I turn towards them again. "Did you sleep well, honey?"

"Um, yes, thank you." I can't look them in the eye, so I focus on the beautiful water instead.

"Do you want some coffee, honey?" Alex is already heading into the kitchen. "Have a seat, I'll bring it out here; Ron needs a refill too."

"Thank you." I sit next to Ron, facing the water still. I can see that he's staring at me though. "Do you know where Max is?"

"He went for a run." Ron looks at his watch, "He should be back any minute." He continues to stare at me, though, so I turn my head to face him directly. "Do you love my son?"

It's so direct, that I don't answer for a second, just sit there with my mouth open, blinking. "Yes...yes, I do." I'm frowning at him. Even though there's no family resemblance, he looks just like Max, strong jawed and intense.

"Good. I can tell that he loves you." He nods his head and picks back up his crossword puzzle from the table. "He's a good man. He deserves to be happy."

"I didn't know how you liked your coffee, so I brought everything out." Alex returns with a big tray of creamer, sugar, sweetener, and a large pot of coffee, so I don't have to reply to Ron. She hands me a mug and fills it up.

I steal a look up at her. I can't reconcile the story from last night. *This sweet woman can't be the same one from that.* Alex is just as nice as my mom. *Hell, even nicer I think.* She looks like she just walked out of an ad, hair perfectly in place, an apron over her fitted shirt and skirt. *This is the second apron I've seen on her.*

I smile at Alex, "Thanks, again." I add a sweetener and cream to the mug. "And thank you for the robe. It was nicer than my one at home."

"I'm glad you were comfy." A timer goes off behind me and Alex jumps up again. "Be right back." She kisses Ron on the cheek before heading inside.

I can hear her moving around the kitchen and hope she won't be long. I don't really want more questions from Ron right now. I busy myself with stirring and sipping.

I jump at a kiss on my head. "Sorry! Didn't see your coffee." Max is standing over me with a crooked smile. I luckily had the mug over the table instead of my lap, so nothing spilled on me. I grab a napkin from the tray and mop up the small mess quickly.

Max sits down next to me, with one hand on the table and one on the back of my chair, facing me. "You were so sound asleep, I didn't want to wake you."

I mumble, "Thanks," and shyly look away, but that only has me looking in Ron's direction as he takes this all in.

Alex comes out baring another tray of small plates, forks, and a platter of large cinnamon rolls. "Now this isn't breakfast, Lucy, but this will tide us over until we can have a proper brunch in town." She distributes plates and I again mumble a thank you.

Max keeps giving me sideways glances, but I avoid looking at anyone directly again, except Alex who sits across from me.

"These are the best cinnabons I've ever had, Mrs. Traeger."

"Please, call us Ron and Alex." Ron answers for her, patting her hand on the table. "Alex is a great cook and world-class baker." He tells a story about a family trip to Italy where Alex ended up teaching a group of local women how to make American-style apple pie.

"We had a lot of fun on that trip. And I think my Italian improved...at least in the kitchen," Alex finishes with a laugh. I take small bites and keep myself chewing or sipping to avoid saying much during the conversation.

Max finally says, "We should get cleaned up if we're going to brunch," and he yanks my chair out a little before I can say anything.

Heading up the stairs in front of him, I feel very conscious of his closeness. He closes the door quickly behind us and I try to move further into the bedroom to get some space between us before turning around.

But he's right in front of me as I turn, "Why are you acting so distant this morning?"

"I'm just...I'm..." I don't know how to put into words how I'm feeling right now; I can only lift my hands at my sides and shrug, turning away. But he catches my hand and pulls me back towards him, taking me into his arms. I can smell his scent more on his partially sweaty t-shirt. It's even muskier and I take a deep breath. *Damn, he smells good.*

He pushes me out to arm's length and holds me there. "Lucy, you need to relax. I know I said a lot last night...and you need some time to process all of it. But today is about a beautiful day on a sun shining lake." He smiles in such a boyish way that I haven't seen before that I can't help but smile back.

"Okay...I'll try."

"Good girl." He kisses me quickly before turning me around to face the bathroom. "Now. Take a shower. I'll wait my turn."

"I'm telling you...it was a mini-mansion...right on the lake." I'm painting my toenails with the phone on speaker, the TV on mute. I'm filling Laura in on my weekend with Max. "...Yes, it was very oo-la-la...if I used that phrase." We laugh together.

"Did you like his parents? Oh shit!" She's painting her toes too on her end. "I smudged."

I hesitate before answering. *I think I could tell Laura almost the whole story, but still...*"Yeah...they were both really nice." I swallow, hesitating again. "They're kinda old fashioned though."

"Like Brady-sitcom-style?"

"Kinda...Alex actually wore not one but two aprons while I was there." We laugh together again.

"Wow. No wonder he's such an ol' fashion guy. He grew up in the Cleaver house." She's laughing harder. I laugh too, but not as hard. I decide not to share anymore.

"It was a really nice time on the lake. We took a speed boat to a restaurant right on the water." She inserts an 'oo-la-la' of her own, "Yeah, I felt very Jackie O-ish as Max sped us around and there was a valet just to help us dock. I was a looong way from Kansas, Toto." I give into more laughter with her.

She tells me I missed a great time Saturday night too. That she went with Tad, Tracy, and Josh to a party on Addison. It got so crowded, she was afraid to go out on the wooden deck. "I'm tellin ya, I could hear the wood splintering."

"Tracy probably jumped up and down on it."

"She did." We're giggling again. It feels good to finally forget about the stress of this week. "Josh had to drag her off it."

"Sorry I missed that."

"No you're not."

"No."

"But seriously...we've missed hanging out with you. We only see you for lunch and happy hour anymore."

"And Romona's. But, yeah. I've missed hangin with you guys too." Almost every night I spend with Max, either here or usually at his place; and it's assumed that I'll stay all weekend at his place. *I can't believe it's only been three weeks and I feel this close to him.*

"So let's make plans. A girls' night out. How bout this Friday?"

"Um...Okay. I'll talk to Max."

"No. You'll *tell* Max that you're going out with us. He can have you to himself on Saturday." She giggles at this, but I sense a little irritation too. She and Tracy have probably talked about my not being around as much lately.

"Okay. Friday night." I try to ignore how saying this tightens my stomach a little. "Let's go dancing!"

"Now you're talking."

Falling asleep without Max is hard. I'm so used to sleeping in his arms, that my bed feels too cold, too empty. I pull his pillow into me and roll over again. *His pillow. Too funny that I think of it that way.*

I sit up, tossing the pillow to the end of the bed. *This is the second night I'm not getting any sleep and it's all his fault!* The clock says 12:30.

I get out of bed, leaving the lights off. Even with the blinds closed, the full moonlight is enough to see clearly by. Putting on my short robe, I move into my kitchen. I have to turn on an under cabinet light to find the tea I want.

Waiting for the chamomile to steep, I open the kitchen door. The new deadbolt turns easily. Max insisted on checking all the doors and windows after my dad pointed out over breakfast that I have another door in the back that needs fixing. He replaced the deadbolt and added locks to all my windows.

I take my tea and sit on my back porch. And I know that Max wouldn't approve of me sitting outside by myself this late.

Well, too bad. I guess you should be here, Max...I'd be asleep then. I stick my tongue out and laugh at myself carrying on imaginary conversations with him. I talk a big talk in my own head. But I know if he were here, I'd be doing whatever he said.

When I asked him earlier tonight why he didn't want to spend the night together again, he said it was because he wanted to give me time to myself. To think. *And I have been thinking. Nonstop...*

Today, I had to stop myself from thinking about what Max said about his parents in the middle of an interview. Tonight, after only meeting Max for drinks and an early dinner, I've been alone, thinking, just like last night.

I've gotten over my initial shock, but what's left is a strange mix of emotions.

After realizing that I couldn't share any of this with Laura or Tracy, I was in a state of panic on Sunday night. It felt too big to deal with on my own. I called my mom. I wasn't going to tell her anything, but I just wanted to hear her voice. It didn't help.

She asked all the right questions, what the Traegers were like, about their house, what we did and ate. She sounded impressed with them, with what I said about them.

Then she quickly changed the subject to PJ and the baby. It's a boy. Everyone's so thrilled. Mom had many miscarriages before she was able to have me. I know family is important to her, to Dad. She brought the conversation back to Max and actually said that maybe he'll propose soon and I'll know the joy of motherhood too.

I couldn't believe she was saying this to me. *She's only met him once.* And I had confessed to her that night that we hadn't been dating that long really. She'd said that it wasn't about how long we'd been together, it was obvious that he really cared about me and he seemed like such a nice gentleman.

Last night on the phone with her, I wanted to say, *yeah, but Mom, that nice gentleman you want me to marry wants to spank me!* I'm laughing still thinking about what her reaction might have been if I'd said that. Instead, what I said was that it was too soon to think about proposals and changed the subject to the weather.

My tea is cold, but I drink it anyway. I need to sleep. My mind needs to shut down. *But I keep thinking...*

Max is a gentleman. A very old fashioned gentleman. He had explained on the ride home more about himself. That previous girlfriends had claimed he was chauvinistic, misogynistic, a bully, possessive, antiquated, abusive. *He used those words.*

And he said he didn't care if that's how today's world would view him. He only cared about being true to himself. And about how I viewed him.

And therein lies the problem...how do *I view him?* How do I reconcile the loving, gentle man who takes such attentive care of me, to the one who makes me wet ordering me around, to the one who scares me with how much he demands? *I just don't know what to think!*

I gulp the last of my tea and put my forehead down on my knee. Sitting on the cold wooden steps, listening to the night move around me, I feel tears starting. My eyes are warm, my chest tight, stomach in a knot, I let out a groan and let the tears come. I only cry for a minute, but I feel better, clearer.

I can't decide everything tonight. But I do know that I love Max. That's why I'm so scared, so confused. I don't want to lose him, but I don't know if I can be what he really wants.

I lift my head up and stare into the moonlit sky. The trees are darkly defined. Not many stars are visible. I feel calmer. I can admit to myself that I'm scared still, but I'm also excited. *I need to see how far Max will take me into this strange new way to think, to be.*

He's everything that I've wanted in a guy; even more, since I've only just realized what it is that I've wanted, what's been missing with past boyfriends. And I know that I've come to terms with how easily I've let Max take over. How much

I've liked that he's taken over, how scared he makes me and how my fear of him is just as exciting as my love for him.

I've been unable to admit to myself before now how much I've changed my thinking for him already. I think first about what would make him happy, pleased with me, before I think about what I want. And this realization makes me feel that same tingle in my stomach, along with a tension in my head. *I still can't believe my own thoughts sometimes.*

I'm wide awake again as I go back inside to try to sleep. I keep my hand on the deadbolt lock for a second. *Good night, Max.* I wish his arms were waiting for me in bed.

32 Him

I knew I needed to give Lucy more space this week. Give her a chance to think about everything. She needs to decide to stay with me on her own. *But on my terms.* So I decided not to push her to talk more to me about everything or to stay the night at my place this week. I didn't even go with to her Wednesday dinner since she said it was just going to be Tracy and Laura.

This has been harder than I thought it would be, giving her space. Since last weekend, I've wanted to do nothing but the opposite. *I want her. Here. With me.*

Taking a deep breath, I check my phone again.

"Man, you need another beer." Mike gets up from the table and heads towards the bar. Since I knew Lucy was out with her friends tonight, I went out with him and Dan after work.

"You really like this girl, don't you?" Dan is smiling at me. He's tried hooking me up with Becca's friends and others since we were roommates. We don't have the same taste in women though. I always joked that he was just sick of double dating with Mike and Steph.

"Yeah. I really do." I take the beer from Mike. "Thanks."

"So you took her up to meet the P's last week? That is a brave girl." Mike is sitting down again and laughing.

"She did great."

"How did Ron like her?" Dan and Mike have both met my parents; Dan even spent a few holidays with us since his family is on the East coast. They are like brothers to me, Dan especially. So he knows how intimidating my dad can be.

I just smile and say, "He really liked her. Gave me his seal of approval."

"Wow. I don't think I got that until we graduated." Mike clinks my bottle.

"You never did." Dan and I say together, laughing.

"Fuck yous." But Mike is laughing too.

"But you've only known her for...what...a month?" Dan is playing big brother again.

"And you were already crying over Becca dumping you for some asshole after a month." Mike laughs when I say this. We like to make fun of Dan and Becca, the old married couple of our group.

"She never dumped me for any asshole, asshole." He throws a peanut at me.

"So when are you two going to make us proud uncles?" Dan flinches at my question, a reaction I haven't seen from him before. *Touchy subject now?*

"We're working on it." This gets a prerequisite nasty comment from Mike and more peanut throwing from Dan. "But Bec is trying to launch her own art in a gallery and I'm trying to support her. So we may hold off on the whole kids thing." He doesn't look me in the eye as he says this. He knows how I feel about family and careers. "For now anyway..." He turns the subject to Mike. "How bout you? When are you going to make Stephanie a poor honest schmuck by marryin her?"

"I'm waiting for her to ask me." We both throw peanuts at him. "We talked about it again, over the Fourth actually." He sits up more. "I don't think she wants to get married. Maybe ever."

"Well, not if you're just going to *talk* about it, schmuck. You have to actually get on a knee and ask her to get an answer." Mike just puts up his hands and grabs his beer to Dan's comment.

"So buy the biggest ring you can find and ask her." I'm on Dan's side. Stephie is not my idea of good wife material, but Mike always seems happy with her.

"I'll ask Stephie after you ask Lucy." Mike is holding his beer out to me.

I know he's making a joke, but I'm serious when I clink and respond, "Deal!"

"You're *that* serious about her?" Dan is leaning forward to look at me closer, big brother once more.

I sit back and swig my beer. "I am." Dan and Mike both shake their heads and laugh at me.

Standing on the curb, it's just Dan and me now. We're standing next to his car. "Hey, I just want to say...Lucy's a nice girl..."

"She is."

"And Bec and I both like her...but take it slow, okay, man?" He pats my chest with the back of his hand hard. "I know you had your heart broken by Nat..."

He doesn't know the details, but he knows that it ended abruptly and I had been really into her. "Lucy's not like that." I cut him off.

"Good. Just...ya know...take it easy."

I smile at him, "I will." I walk away before he can say anything more.

33 Her

"Do you need a cab, Lucy?" The big bouncer at the entrance stops me before I head up the stairs to the street.

"Oh...uh...no thanks." I wave as I quickly walk by their table.

This has been an odd night. It's been an odd week.

Max has been staying away. He still thinks I need some space. I haven't shared with him any of my thoughts, any of the insights I've had this week about how I feel about him and what he said. I still haven't slept much either without him, but I'm hoping this weekend we can talk more and he'll spend the night again.

I was grateful that I didn't have to explain his coming along on Wednesday, though. Tracy would've made a big deal out of me not standing up to him and saying he wasn't invited along to a girl's night. And I know that if he had pushed to be there, I *wouldn't* have stood up to him.

It felt nice to have the girls-only dinner again. I like Josh and Tad is sweet, but they can be immature sometimes. And Tracy gets bolder with Josh around, laughing and talking louder, making out in the hall outside the bathroom.

It was also a relief when I told Max about our Friday night plans, he wasn't upset at all. He just insisted that we go to a club that's a part of the LPE Group. *I didn't realize how different tonight was going to be though.*

From the moment we got in line to get into Club French, I was treated like a star. A bouncer came over to me and asked my name, then he led us by the long line right into the club. We didn't even have to pay to get in. He introduced me to another guy at the bottom of the stairs and he showed us to a table in the roped off VIP section.

Tracy and Laura just followed along. Once we were seated, they took turns saying "Oo-la-la" and poking at me. A bartender came over with a bottle of champagne and a bucket. He didn't even say anything, just opened the bottle. More Oo-la-la's.

We danced and drank like usual, but I felt very conspicuous. Like all the bouncers and bartenders knew who I was and were keeping an eye on us. If a guy came up to talk to us, I swear the bouncers seemed closer, ready to step in.

Tracy started saying that Max was keeping tabs on me, but Laura just said it was sweet of him to treat us to a night out like this. I didn't tell them that Max had made me promise to leave by midnight, too. I just said that I was feeling tired and ready to go.

They both wanted to stay, which was fine with me, but Tracy kept joking that I was leaving to be with Max and it was supposed to be our night out. Laura just laughed and said,

"Don't do anything I wouldn't do. Wait, don't do anything Tracy *would* do!" I left with them laughing and pushing each other. Looking back, I could see another bottle of champagne being delivered to them.

On the street I turn towards the corner, but am stopped by a yell. "Lucy?"

"Jeff?" He's walking towards me. "What are you doing here?"

"Max wanted me to make sure you make it home okay." He extends his arm back the way he came and I can see the car parked.

"Oh...Okay, thanks." I walk back and let him open the door for me.

In the car, I look at my phone for the bazillionth time tonight. *No call or text from Max.* Just the one he sent at 6:00, "have fun tonight. be safe!" *I know it's late, but he'd want me to call.*

Max picks up on the first ring. "Hey."

"Hey yourself." I'm excited to hear his voice. I've really missed spending so much time with him, falling asleep with him. "I'm heading home, just wanted to say goodnight."

"Good girl. It's midnight on the dot. Are you with Jeff?"

"Yes. Thank you for the ride. And for everything tonight. Tracy and Laura were really impressed with our star treatment." I put my feet up on the seat and relax. It no longer feels weird to have a private driver.

"Good. I'm glad you had fun." He pauses before asking, "Were you a good girl tonight?"

My stomach tightens and I feel the familiar tingle in my pussy from his deep voice. "...Yes..."

"You didn't over drink...you didn't flirt with anyone..."

"No. I was very good." I laugh self-consciously. "I danced my as...*butt*...off though." I stop myself from cursing, smiling that Max is probably smiling on his end too.

"But I like your ass just the way it is." I can hear the smile. *And the desire.*

I open my eyes as we stop at a light and realize that we're not heading in the right direction. "Hey. Did you tell Jeff to take me to your place?"

"Yes. I've missed you."

"Good. I've missed you too."

"And I want to make sure that you've been a good girl..." Same tingling from my stomach down to my pussy at his voice.

"Well...I'll be happy to see you. I've missed sleeping in your arms."

"You'll be in them in a minute, baby."

34 Him

I open the door and grab her arm, yanking her into my chest. She's laughing. "You *have* missed me."

"Yes." I growl this into her hair, breathing in her perfume.

"*I've* missed you." She stands on tip-toe and kisses me. I can see that she's wearing a tight dress, not one of my favorites, her body too on display.

"I thought you said you were a good girl tonight." She freezes in my arms.

"I was." She sounds a little defiant. *But only a little.*

"*That's* what you chose to wear out with your friends?" We've already had several talks about how I expect her to dress around me.

She looks down at herself and back up to me. The look of guilt is gorgeous, eyes wide, mouth soft. "I like this dress."

She's trying to kiss me again, but I lean my head back a little so she can't reach my face. "And I bet every guy there liked it too."

She stands flat again, only her eyes raised to me, her hands behind her back on my arms. She knows I like how small she is, how sexy she looks this way. "Are you jealous?" She has a half-smile, a laugh wanting to escape.

I wait until she lifts her chin up towards me, no longer confident in her sexiness. She's searching my face, the guilty look back in place on hers. She swallows hard, her throat moving up and down.

"No. Not jealous." I squeeze her to me, lifting her off the ground back onto her tip-toes. "Possessive." She starts to smile, but stops before it reaches her eyes. She's searching my face again. "You belong to *me*." She completes her smile at this.

I push her away. "Take off that dress." I allow some anger into my voice. "Now!" She jumps in place a little and reaches behind her to unzip. I grab her shoulders and twist her around. Putting my hands at the base of her neck, I rip the dress down the middle, tearing the zipper apart. She half gasps, half cries out.

I push her slightly towards the wall. "Take it off." She moves with her hands shaking and pushes the sleeves down her arms, stepping out of the dress without facing me, standing close to the wall. "Turn around." She slowly pivots to me, her breathing short, eyes down, hands crossed in front of her pussy. *I like watching her like this.*

She finally takes a deep breath, her ribs pushed out, tits pushed up. She raises her chin and meets my eyes. "You didn't have to tear it." She's trying to sound unashamed, but I can see the fear in her eyes. I wait until she blinks away all defiance, leaving just the fear and need to please.

"You won't be wearing that again." I take a step towards her and she takes an involuntary step back; the wall stops her from moving further. I smile, the steel staying in my eyes, the fear in hers.

I reach out my hand to cup her face and enjoy how she flinches away. I pull her towards me with my hand on the back of her neck. She keeps her eyes on me and doesn't move her hands. *The wary prey.* But when I kiss her, she melts into me, her body relaxing and hands going around me to claw my back. I hiss and bite her lower lip so she stops.

I take her hand and lead her into the bedroom. She quietly follows. *The willing prey now.*

We stand facing each other next to the bed. I reach around her and undo her bra, pulling the straps down gently. She remains still and looking into my eyes. I gently push her boy shorts down and she steps out of these towards me.

She pushes my t-shirt up and I help her getting it over my head. She pushes my sweatshorts down, taking my boxers with them. She stands with her arms at her sides, waiting for me to make the next move.

I rub my hands up her arms. My touch is smooth and almost tickling her. I gently take the weight of her tits into my hands. Her breathing is picking up again. I squeeze hard. Her eyes open wide, her breath in sharp. She puts her hands over mine. I only shake my head at her, giving her a warning look. She slowly drops her hands to her side again. I continue squeezing until she lowers her eyes. I move my fingers to her nipples. I start to pinch; her eyes jerk up to mine again; I pinch harder. Her eyes plead. I pinch harder. She squeaks out a cry. As I let go, she gulps a breath in.

I pick her up by her arms and throw her onto the bed. I'm on top of her before she stops bouncing, straddling her hips. I grab her wrists and pull them over her head, crushing them with my weight. "...Max...?" She's pleading.

"Keep quiet, baby." I'm harder at the light moan, her only response. I hold her wrists down with my left hand, letting my right hand travel over her. Roughly grabbing her hair and twisting her head to the right, I bite her neck. She squeaks and moans again.

My hand continues to travel down her, pinching one nipple, not having to pinch hard to elicit a cry. I put my hand between her legs, pushing roughly, since my legs are still keeping hers together.

She's so wet. I shove three fingers into her, jabbing her pussy with my knuckles. Her cry is a little louder now, against my chest. I pull her clit with two of my fingers, pinching and pulling until her moan is long and continuous. Her hips are bucking against me, my cock pressed into one.

I can't wait any longer. Keeping her legs together, I shove my cock into her wet pussy. My next thrust is slower, pushing up, feeling my full length against her bone as I go in and out. I drag her clit down with my cock and her moan deepens. I continue this slow pace, with her hips pushing her clit into me at the beginning of each thrust. When I come, I stay deep in her and grind her clit with my finger as she finishes coming on me.

I slide to her side, releasing her wrists. She wraps herself around me, pressing her body along my side.

Her breathing is starting to even into sleep. I quietly kiss her head, "You do belong to me, Lucy." I put my hand in her hair and press her head against my chest more. "And I have missed you this week." She turns her face up to me. "I don't want to spend any time apart again. I've given you all the time to think that you're going to get from me."

She lowers her face again and presses into me more, "Okay," is her meek reply.

I wake to the sounds of cooking in my kitchen. *And burnt toast?* In just my boxers, I go see what Lucy is making.

She is so beautiful, moving between the stove and counter, humming to herself, my t-shirt hanging to her knees. She jumps when she sees me leaning against the wall. "Morning, sweetie." She comes over and gives me a big hug, before turning back to the stove. "I made coffee. Probably not as strong as you like though." She laughs.

"I wasn't sure you could cook." I laugh too, pouring coffee into the mug she left out for me.

"Ha! I can make breakfast...and spaghetti." She is putting scrambled eggs on a plate next to sausage patties.

"So long as you don't make spaghetti for breakfast..." I take a plate from her. "Thanks."

"Ha ha." She turns to the toaster and pulls out the burnt pieces. "Oops. Apparently I'm not good with your fancy toaster, though. Sorry. I can make some more real quick..."

I stop her. "This is fine." We take our plates to the dining table. "You must've been up early. I didn't hear you wake up."

"I finally got some sleep." She takes a bite before adding, "I haven't slept well all week without you, ya know." She says this accusingly and with a pout.

"Me neither." I finish a patty. "This is really good, Lucy. You'll have to start making breakfast every morning." I wink at her. She just smiles and keeps eating. I finally do what I've been waiting until today for, "Did you think? About us...like I told you to?"

She looks down at her plate, fork moving eggs around, but not eating. Shyly, "...Yes."

"And what did you think?" I keep eating with my eyes on her.

She's fidgeting with her napkin, finally putting it in her lap before she speaks. Sitting back and looking directly at me, "I love you."

I smile. *A good start.* "I love you." I wait for her to continue.

"And..." She takes a deep breath looking up to my ceiling before meeting my eyes again, "and I want to be with you."

Good. "...On my terms?"

She is swallowing hard again, eyes not blinking. "...Yes..." I can tell she's twisting her napkin in her lap again.

"You understand that this means things will change between us?" I keep my hands flat on the sides of my forgotten breakfast.

"I think so..." Her voice is tiny, eyes wet from not blinking still. She finally lowers her eyes. "I don't really know what you mean..." She looks back up to me and her eyes are still wet, but no tears fall. "All I know is I trust you. And I want to be what you want."

I push my chair back and put out my arm. She jumps onto my lap quickly, pulling herself into a ball. I hold her close, my arm around her waist and knees.

"You've made me very happy, Lucy."

35 Him

Rosa comes over to great me with a big hug as I enter the small restaurant. "They're back there." She thumbs behind her. "Just follow the giggling."

I can hear Tracy. She's laughing loudly in the middle of a story. "...And then this big-ass bouncer comes out of nowhere and pushes these assholes off the dance floor. It was like Lucy had a fuckin' entourage..."

I come around the corner just as Lucy is laughing and saying, "It was *not* a fuckin' entourage." And Laura is adding, "You're just jealous, bitch," at the same time. Josh and Tad are laughing along with them.

I put my hand on Lucy's chair and she jumps up. "Oh, good. You made it." She sits back down as I hold her seat. "I wasn't sure your meeting was going to finish in time..." Her smile freezes a little, in response to my stony glare at her.

I turn towards the table, though, and put on a half-smile for everyone. "I wouldn't miss Rosa's cooking."

Tracy tells me to call her Romona, "She hates it." *I'm beginning not to like this girl.* "I was just telling Josh and Tad what a wonderful night we had out thanks to you. All Lucy had to do was snap her fingers and we were floating in champagne."

"I would hope no one was snapping their fingers at anyone." I say this with a smile, but keep my voice even and edgy.

Lucy puts her hand on my arm and says quietly, "No. Of course not."

"No. We just wanted to say thanks...it was a lot of fun to be pampered for the night." *Laura is a sweet girl.*

Tad pokes her side making her laugh loudly, "What? You don't call buying you a cheeseburger Sunday pamperin you?" The table laughs, Lucy quieter than the others.

Good. She gets that I'm upset with her, even if she doesn't know why. Yet.

Lucy leans over to me and says quietly, "I ordered Puttanesca for us..." She looks at me like a puppy waiting for a treat, all hopeful.

"Good." I keep my hand on her leg under the table, pinching her until she puts her hand over mine. I stop her from rubbing the spot by flattening my hand back over hers. She keeps looking at me, but I ignore her and carry on a conversation with Tad about his softball team's winning streak. "I belonged to a softball league a few years ago. Let me know if you ever need a filler."

Before heading to the car, I pull Lucy back from her friends. Her eyes open wide in surprise at the suddenness. "I want you to be silent on the ride home. Not a *word* until we get there." She only nods slowly in response to my gritted teeth command.

"Good night, Max. Lucy, you get some rest." Rosa is waving from the door.

Tracy yells back, "Where's our love?"

"Good night, Trouble!" But Rosa is blowing her a kiss, heading back inside as I close my door.

I take Lucy's hand and kiss her palm. With her head lowered, eyes raised, she Mona-Lisa smiles at me, but doesn't say anything. *Good.*

Lucy remains quiet in the elevator, holding my hand and rubbing with her thumb, in an attempt to get me to smile back at her.

I open the door and step aside to let her in. She walks a few steps as I just calmly watch her. I haven't spoken either since leaving the restaurant. I drop my keys on the table. And move towards her in two long strides.

Turning around Lucy finally says what her eyes have been questioning all night, "Max, why are you so…" She doesn't get the rest out.

I slap the side of her face, hard. She falters back a step into the wall, putting both hands up to cover the left side of her face, cowering from me.

"Oh my God." She stares at me, searching my face, not moving.

I wait.

I need to see her reaction. What she does next will determine so much between us. *No matter how much we've talked, tonight decides our fate.*

"You...you. Oh my God." She lowers her head and moves her hands to hide her whole face.

I wait.

Inches from her, I don't move. When she looks up, there's a dawning mix of anger and fear on her face. *And what I've been hoping for. Guilt.*

I wait.

"Why...?" It's more a breath. "...What...?" She's searching my face for an explanation. *Good.*

I don't move, but speak slowly and with all the anger I feel in my voice. "What did I tell you about your language?"

She just swallows and blinks at me with the same mixed look, with a frown starting on her face.

I wait.

She shakes her head slightly and lowers her hands. I slap her again, just as hard. Her hands go up to her face once more and stay there. When she opens them, her eyes have the beginning of tears. Her look is fear. And more guilt. *Good.* My cock thickens at the sight of her.

"...Max..." She stops, hands still on her face, a tear falling over her knuckles, her eyes pleading.

"I told you to watch your mouth. Didn't I?" I keep my voice steady and slow again.

"You...I...didn't..." She's shaking her head again.

"I heard you when I got to the restaurant, Lucy."

I wait.

Her eyes dart between mine for what feels like a full minute. She puts her one hand out against my chest, warding me off, pleading with me. "I didn't...I...I didn't know you were there..."

"And that's your excuse?" I yell this and laugh cruelly. She flinches nicely, her hand shaking slightly on my chest. Her eyes go towards the door.

"What... You wanna go?" I grab her arm off my chest and yank her towards the door one step before yanking her back against the wall, shoving her hard into it.

Both her hands go up to my chest now. I take a small step away from her, so she drops them to her sides. "If you want to go, then go." Her head jerks up to mine. "Just understand this, little girl...if you walk out that door, there will be *no* coming back." I'm glad her hand isn't on my chest now. She'd feel my heart beating too quickly.

If she turns towards the door now...I will have to let her go. And I would be heartbroken. *But I need to let her make this one decision. She has to stay on her own. She has to take what I demand, what I've done.*

I wait.

She keeps looking into my eyes before finally more tears well up. Her face crumbles and she looks down, hair veiling her face.

And I know she's mine. I'm through waiting.

"Do you want to go?" I say it quieter, but with the same edge. She only shakes her head, still lowered.

"Look at me!" Her head jerks up at the sharpness. "Answer me. Do you want to leave?" I say it sharp as a knife over the last word. She cowers again.

"...No..." It's a squeak, hardly a sound.

"No. You answer me with respect, Lucy. Say 'No, *Sir*.'" I say this only a little softer, still slowly.

She squeaks out "...No...Sir..." still staring at me, tears sliding down her cheeks beautifully as she blinks.

I step closer to her and she puts her hands up again, fear blanching her cheeks. My cock is so hard, I want to take her right now.

"Put your hands behind your back." But I move them there for her. She's pliant and shaking now. Her head lowers almost to my chest. "When I'm disciplining you, Lucy, you'll keep your hands out of the way."

She looks up, through wet lashes. "Max...please..." My cock moves.

"Shhh..." I stroke the right side of her head and kiss her forehead. "It's almost over, baby." I'm tender when I say this, only a little edge to my voice.

I stand taller and Lucy tenses again. *She responds so easily.* "You know I don't want you to curse." I allow the anger to seep back into my voice.

She hesitates before saying so quietly that I almost don't hear her, "Yes....Sir."

"And yet you did it anyway..." My anger is heating again, remembering how she sounded with all her friends laughing at her foul mouth.

"I...I didn't know you were there..." She says this as a plea this time.

"That's no excuse, Lucy. You'll behave how I tell you to, whether I'm there or not!"

"Okay." She says this quickly, with her whole body tensing away from me, pressing against the wall. I push into her slightly and she quickly adds, "...Sir."

I relax slightly and she almost falls onto my chest, burying herself against me. I hold the side of her face with my left hand, forcing her to look at me again. "Lucy." I stop to admire the look of fear and pleading in her eyes. "I'm going to slap you one more time." I speak slowly. She tries to shake her head, but my hand keeps her still. "Stop!" Her body shakes against me, but she stops moving her head.

"I want you to remember this lesson." Her mouth opens like she's going to say something, but doesn't. "I'm going to slap you again," I repeat, looking slowly between her eyes. "And if you're a good girl...keep your hands behind your back...and don't move...this will all be over." I give her a second to think about what I've said. A look of greater fear darkens her eyes to a deep blue. "Do you understand me?" She can only nod, her mouth opening, but no sound coming out, her breath shallow. "Good."

I quickly take a small step back and slap her. Harder this time. *I want to leave a mark on her.*

Lucy cries out, bouncing against the wall. I catch her as she bounces back to me, holding her to me before she can move, taking her arms and putting them around my shoulders. She nearly collapses, crying and shaking. Picking her up, I carry her into the bedroom. She's buried the left side of her face into my chest, the rest completely covered by her hair.

The sound of her soft hiccupping cries moves my cock again and I lower her legs to the floor, pressing her into me.

36 Her

My face is on fire and numb at the same time, pressed into his chest. I don't think I've breathed for the last ten minutes and hiccups mix with my sobbing.

I'm rubbery and don't trust my legs to hold me. Max keeps his arms tight around me. *I can't move.* But my brain is on hyper-load.

It's replaying everything like in a movie. It's all in slow motion, in a loop. I keep seeing his hand coming up to my face, his eyes behind so stern, his mouth and jaw so set.

I've only been slapped once before. My mom was so scared when I ran out into the street when I was five; she almost yanked my arm out and slapped me before hugging me to her legs, crying.

This was different. This wasn't a knee-jerk reaction. Max was angry. He was very angry, stewing in anger all night. But he was also controlled. He could've really hurt me, but instead he only slapped me.

Oh, God. Only *slapped me? I must be losing my mind.*

But even as I think this, I can feel the stomach-to-pussy stabbing sensation again. After he slapped me the first time, I was afraid he would just keep hitting me. When he didn't, I was confused. I felt shattered and scared, but his control and voice also sent that shockwave through me, down, making me wet. I couldn't think. *My brain said run, my body said stay, my heart...my heart was afraid to decide.*

I knew he was angry all night. I could feel his coldness. But he wasn't distant. He kept his hands on me. I can still feel where he pinched me. His touch had been rough before, grabbing me, holding me down; but this time it was around other people, my friends. *I couldn't believe he sat there, looking so calm, talking...all the while pinching me. And I didn't say anything.*

That was the first ping of shock to my pussy. I felt lightheaded after that, like I couldn't concentrate on anything but Max, hardly touching my food. Rosa asked if I wasn't feeling well and he answered for me that I was just tired.

When he commanded me not to speak...*Oh, God, commanded me!*...I was wet the whole ride home. In this state of confusion.

I thought we might argue in his apartment about whatever he was mad at, then make up. *It even crossed my mind that he might want to spank me.* That thought made it even harder to stay quiet. I almost laughed out loud once. *But I didn't expect him to slap me.* My head spins again.

37 Him

I continue holding her up, her forehead pressed down against my chest. She clings to my arms.

Slowly her sobbing and hiccups taper off. She laughs out loud, short and shaky. *Not a sound I was expecting to hear tonight. I hope she isn't getting hysterical.*

I lift her chin to my face. She slowly raises her eyes, the most beautiful light blue, the lids a little red from crying.

"Let me see you." She blinks the last of her tears away as I turn her face to the right. "You'll have a mark." She tries to jerk her head away, but I hold her in place. Only her eyes dart to me, the fear back in an instant. "You can look in a minute." I let go of her face, putting my hand back around her waist. She's still shaking a little. She sniffs and starts to lower her head again.

"You have one more thing to do before you can wipe your face and nose." Her head jerks back up. *I love how responsive she is, how open she is. Her eyes tell me so much...fear, hope, and that beautiful look of shame again.*

"You have to say you're sorry for misbehaving." She smiles for a second and I think she might laugh in hysteria again, but quickly her face freezes into shock and fear instead.

Swallowing hard first, "...I'm...sorry..." She haltingly gets this out, but I'm proud of her for not looking down while saying it. *She's learning already.*

"Good girl. Go wash your face and blow your nose." I let go of her, but steady her before she leaves my arms.

38 Her

I turn the water off and pat my face dry. I'm gentle with the left side. I haven't really looked yet.

Just as I pull my hair back and turn towards the mirror, the door opens. I jump and gasp, dropping my hands to the counter to avoid falling forward into the sink.

Max leans against the doorway, just looking at me calmly, his arms crossed in front. The look on his face is unreadable, soft, but with an edge that sends warning shocks to my stomach again.

He doesn't say anything, only nods toward the mirror. I turn my head back, looking at him in reflection now. I slowly raise my hands to my hair again, my eyes drawn to a small red mark on my cheekbone, almost the size of one of his fingers, and the start of a small bruise under my jawline. I'm a little puffy all over from crying, but especially on the left side.

I can't look away. I see Max move towards me, but I remain statue, only my eyes moving with him. He stands right behind me. His face in full view, his body outlining mine. He takes a deep breath, but doesn't say anything again.

Finally, he reaches forward and lowers my arms from behind. My hair falls to cover my jaw, but not the mark on my cheek. I swallow hard.

"Aren't you...Aren't you going to say something? Say you're sorry?" My voice is extra high, shaky.

Max laughs once; it echoes on the marble. "No." I stare in disbelief into his eyes.

And slowly I realize that I didn't expect him to be sorry. *Maybe didn't even want him to be?* I know he expects me to be the one who is ashamed. *And I am*. My mind is still reeling. But my heart and body have already decided.

He puts his hands slowly on my hips, not taking his eyes from mine in the mirror.

39 Him

She puts her hands over mine and I speak again, "No. Keep them on the counter." She obeys quickly.

I rub my hands down her sides, reaching the end of her skirt and bunching it up around her waist. She is pushed forward with this motion and her ass arches up to me more. I put one arm around her front, forcing her hips up, forcing her to tip-toe. She says nothing, but her eyes are very hungry.

With my other hand, I pull my own pants and boxers down, letting them fall to my ankles. She gasps as I yank her thong down next. It stops at mid-thigh. I force her knees apart with my hand, the thong cutting into her legs.

Her pussy is dripping wet already, lips swollen and pulsing with her heartbeat. My slightest touch has her moaning and pressing herself into my fingers. I know I'm not going to be able to wait this time.

I shove into her as hard as I can, holding her hips up so she's almost off the floor. She falls forward, hands slapping the mirror to steady herself. Her moan is deep and animal, matching mine. She pushes back against the mirror, her moans not stopping. I know this deep is hurting her, but I keep her hips locked against me, pushing and pulling her with quick thrusts. She's bucking as she comes. I let go of her hips and push into her one more time, coming deep inside her.

I stay with my hand on her back, panting with her. I can't see her face with her head down again, hands still on the mirror. She starts to shake. I slowly take my cock out of her, the feel of her movements causing a rise again.

She turns around and slams herself into my arms, crying hard against me. I hold her until she calms more. Finally, she lifts her face to mine.

"I love you." I kiss her cheeks, tasting the saltiness of her tears.

She sniffs. "I love you too, Max."

40 Her

My wake up alarm goes off somewhere. I roll over, the weight of Max's arm sliding with me. I move one leg over the edge of the bed. Max pulls me back into his side.

"No." He growls sleepily. "Stay."

I snuggle back for a second. "I have to get my phone..."

He just shakes his head, eyes still not open. "You have to stay right where you are."

We lay like this for a little longer, before he growls again louder. "All right! Go shut that off."

I laugh at him, eyes still not open, hands over his ears. I sit up and reach for the shirt I wore last night, now on the floor. He grabs my arm, startling me, "No shirt. You're coming right back here."

I smile as I stand up. "I have to pee..."

"You heard me. Come right back here." He has a relaxed smile, turned on his side towards me, a sheet wrapped loosely around his waist. I can see his cock clearly outlined and stiff. After last night, even the slight sharpness in his voice makes my heart beat faster, though.

I hurry out to the hall, finding my purse and phone on the table. I shut off the alarm and turn back, catching sight of myself in the mirror.

My left cheek is a deeper red now. I turn my face to the side and can see the bruise under my jaw is also darker. And I have a small bruise on my thigh.

Max is in the same position when I slowly walk back into the bedroom. He pats the bed next to him. But I stay just inside the doorway, my tits somewhat covered by my hair, my hands covering between my legs. Nonetheless, I feel very exposed.

In a small voice, "I should head home. I don't have any makeup here." I gesture quickly towards my face, but drop my hand back down just as fast. "And I need to get to the office early today."

He doesn't move, just stays staring at me with his head supported by his bent elbow. I start to walk towards the bathroom.

"Come here, Lucy." I stop in mid-stride. His voice has that more dangerous edge from last night. My stomach hurts from the need to pee mixing with that excitement in my pussy again. I turn around slowly and, letting out a shaky breath, I walk over to the edge of the bed just as slowly. *I am in that movie again. Except now I'm the one thing moving in slow motion.*

He looks at the side of my face and pats the bed once. I sit. His hand is in slow motion too, reaching out and pulling me back into his side again. I'm stiff and not moving.

"We'll stay in bed today." He kisses the back of my head. I can feel his cock hard against me.

Again in a small voice, "I have to go to work..." I'm feeling so confused. Seeing my face bruised made me afraid of him again. *It made me feel...I don't even know...this other sensation...a hunger for him that makes me wet.* I should be running out of here, but instead I feel his warmth and feel safer.

He kisses my head again. "We're playing hooky. You're not leaving." His tone is final, warning me not to say anything more.

"No one can see me like this," I whisper. I want him to say something about my face, about what he did to me. My anger and fear resurface. I move to face him, my body stretched out next to his, but leaving a space between us. I put my hands on his chest to keep the distance. "Look at what you did to my face, Max..."

He looks into my eyes, like he's looking for something. "Watch your tone, Lucy." *Damn. That instant pussy pulsing...what has happened to me?* I look down at my hands, unable to keep his stare, then back up pleading with my eyes for him to answer me.

He pushes my hair away from my face on the right side, but I can see him scrutinizing the left side again. The cheek mark is probably just visible to him from his angle.

"I think you're beautiful." His voice hasn't changed, the same even-toned, depth with a hint of warning.

I smile, then stop, then try again, nervous. "But...?"

"But nothing. I wanted to leave a mark on you." He again looks like he's looking for something in my expression. I realize he's gauging my reactions and again feel a flutter in my stomach. *He's so calm and in control and my head is so not in control right now.*

"You...you meant...to give me a bruise?" I'm completely stiff, my hands cold on his chest.

"Yes." He covers my hands with his. I flinch away from his sudden movement and see him smile in response. "I wanted to leave you with a mark last night. As a reminder for you of what disobeying me will get you."

I stay stiff and quiet, unsure of what to do or say. *Hell, I'm unsure of what I want to do or say!*

Jump out of bed? Hit him and scratch his eyes out? Crawl into his arms and beg his forgiveness? Bury my head in his chest and cry again?

I can only manage a shuttering breath in and out. My head is light again.

"Lucy." His voice brings me out of myself. I open my eyes. "I need you to understand. This is how it's going to be...from now on." He speaks slowly to me, like I'm a child he's teaching. I still have a hard time following his words. *Good thing I'm already lying down!*

"Do you understand that?"

"Yes." It's a stuttered word, my whole body shaking with it. I want him to put his arms around me, to cover me with his warmth, but he doesn't move.

"Is that how you answer me?" Warning voice...fluttering stomach.

And I know that the hungry feeling for him has won against all my other sensible thoughts. I give in to what I need...him.

"Yes...Sir." And my whisper is rewarded with his warmth.

Max and Lucy continue their story in

True Beginnings.

1 Him

We're different. Wednesday night, yesterday, it changed everything between us. *It clarified everything.*

I smile thinking of how Lucy was yesterday. *A shaky start, but a good beginning for us.* She was so hesitant, trying to still hold back. She wasn't ready to embrace her new life with me, not completely, not yet. *She was almost there, though.* I'm getting her the rest of the way there.

Yesterday, she was able to give in to what she really wants, submit to her true feelings. We had a nice day together, playing hooky, staying in my bed, ordering food in, and keeping the world out.

I knew seeing her face in a mirror would bring back a little of her fear and maybe some of her anger. She had to get used to seeing herself as mine. That I could do as I like to her, punish her how I want, and she'd accept it. Yesterday, she started to do this...*with my help.*

But today is the true start. Today the world is let back in; rather, Lucy has to face her world from her newly defined role with me. *Today is an important first step for us.*

I hear her bare feet on the tile in her kitchen, but I keep my eyes closed. "Are you going to stay in bed all day, again, ya bum?"

I only open one eye. Lucy is standing with her hands on her hips. She has a bra and thong on, her short robe open in the front, her blonde hair falling in wet ringlets past her shoulders. She also already has on a lot of makeup. It's why I had agreed to sleeping here last night, instead of at my place, so she could cover the red mark on her cheek and bruise under her jaw for work today.

I smile at her and still with only one eye open put my arm out for her to come to me.

She shakes her head and crosses her arms in front. "Oh, no...I'm not getting back in bed with you. We have to go to work today."

I stop smiling and harden my look. She instantly moves to crawl in bed, snuggling in with her back to me. *Things are definitely different between us*. "Good girl." I kiss her head and feel her relax a little more. "Let me see you."

She knows what I mean. Slowly, she rolls over to face me, putting her hands on my chest. I push her hair away from the left side of her face. Taking hold of her chin, I gently turn her face more. Both marks are well covered. The redness on her cheek is already fading, spreading into a lighter shade; the bruise along her jaw isn't as hidden, the blue of the center showing a little, the surrounding yellow covered only a little better. *But her thick hair will cover this*.

I actually *like* seeing the small bruises on her. I worry that this makes me a monster. *I hope my own past won't work its way into our future*. But I know that my love for

Lucy is stronger than any violence or anger I've been through.

"You're beautiful." I kiss her nose. She finally raises her eyes to me.

"You...you can't see anything, Max?" She's shaky still. In the dark before falling asleep, she had said she was afraid of her friends seeing something at work, that she wouldn't know what to say to them. I told her not to worry about it. We could stay home together one more day and then she'd have the whole weekend in between the next time she needed to see anyone from work if she wanted. It was her choice.

"No. You did a good job, baby." I kiss her and she melts into me more, relieved. "Just keep your hair down if you don't want anyone to ask you any questions." She stiffens again.

"So you *can* see something?" A hint of defiance has creeped back in her eyes. She drops this quickly though. Her eyes show only fear when she asks, "Aren't *you* afraid of someone asking me about my face?" The shakiness increased in her voice to end in more of a whine.

"No."

She searches my face, my eyes. I don't say more just calmly look back at her. Lucy finally closes her mouth and swallows hard, before blurting out, "Why not?"

I speak slowly. *This is important for her to understand and I need to be clear with her about this part from the very beginning.* Despite my own fears about my anger and my past, this is important for us going forward. "Because if anyone asks you, you'll have to say what happened. Won't you?" The bewildered look on her face again, mouth opening, then closing. I wait until she only nods, slowly. *Good.*

"And what happened...is you misbehaved. Didn't you?" I pause again, waiting longer for her to slowly nod a tiny bit. Her eyes show a hint of the shame that made them so beautifully full of tears Wednesday night. "And I had to punish you. Didn't I?" The pause this time stretches longer. Her hands grow warm on my chest, her cheeks flaring red. She lowers her eyes before imperceptibly nodding.

"Answer me, Lucy." Her head jerks up quickly. *Good girl.*

Her responsiveness to the nuances of my voice and facial changes is still a marvel to me. I only added the slightest amount of sharpness and she is quick to reply, "Yes, Sir...." *She's learning.*

"Lucy, I'll make a lot of promises to you. And I will *always* keep my promises." She nods, relaxing. "I *will* discipline you. And my punishments *will* hurt." I wait for her to relax again. "I will even leave marks on you sometimes to help you remember to be my good girl long after a punishment." I rub her hair; her eyes can't meet mine. "But I will never *harm* you." She looks up questioning now. "I won't damage you. Do you understand?"

She is searching my eyes again. "I think so…"

"I want you to know that you're safe with me. To not question that part."

"I know that, Max."

"Good." I give her a small kiss on her cheek. "I *want* you to be afraid of making me angry…this will help you to remember how to behave." She only nods, a little look of fear and guilt added to her searching eyes. "But I don't want you to be afraid of me truly hurting you. I will never do anything to you…that can't heal without damage." I falter on how to make this clearer without scaring her more. *I want to reassure her, not frighten her this morning.*

She takes her time answering, swallowing several times, "I knew from what you said before…about your family, your beliefs…that you might…that you *would*...do *something* if you were angry with me." She swallows more. Her chin lifts a bit and her eyes focus on mine, "But I know that you love me, Max. And I know that I love you. And I know that I trust you."

I kiss her again and she is even more eager to kiss me back. "You better get ready for work...unless you want to stay with me today again?" I tenderly pull her hair forward, over her shoulder.

"No. No, I'll be okay." I let her get out of bed and watch her select a short-sleeved dress out of her closet. She turns to face me with the dress in front of her, "Do you like this one?" The blue of her eyes pop even more against the pale blue of the dress. She looks anxious to please me. It's one of the ones we bought together.

I give her a big smile, "It's perfect." We're meeting a few of my friends for dinner tonight right after work. I don't know if she remembers this with all that has happened over the last two days. "Remember, we're going to dinner tonight...?"

Her eyes answer before she does, "Oh! ...I forgot..."
The look of apprehension is back. She just takes her dress
and heads towards the kitchen and attached bathroom. At the
end of the bed, though, she turns back to me, "You don't
really want me to say any of that, do you...I mean...you want
me to make something up...if anyone asks...?"

"No, Lucy, I expect you to say exactly what I said."
She starts to laugh, but stops herself. Again, she's very quick
to respond to the subtle changes in my look. "You earned
those marks, little girl. For misbehaving. And I won't have
you lying about how you got them."